HER LAST TOMORROW

ADAM CROFT

Published by Thomas & Mercer, Seattle

www.apub.com

ISBN-13: 9781503940093
ISBN-10: 1503940098

Cover design by Lisa Horton

Printed in the United States of America

HER LAST TOMORROW

HER LAST TOMORROW

1

NICK

The combination of burnt toast and cold coffee has never been my favourite, but it's growing on me. It does that after a while.

I've given up even bothering to scrape the black bits off the toast, but the coffee still goes in the microwave. Iced coffee I can understand, but lukewarm coffee might as well be dog's piss. Having to live off caffeine is bad enough, so it might as well taste good in the process.

The microwave bleeps three times to tell me it's done, the shrill sound piercing through my skull as I chomp down on another bite of toast, sending large black chunks crumbling to the floor.

The nagging thought at the forefront of my mind is that this damn book is never going to be finished. It'll be a year next week since I started writing it, and I'm already on my third deadline. Pete tells me it's my last deadline. I know he's serious this time. I'm really starting to wonder if it might just be better to scrap the whole thing and run with another idea. Any book's better than no book.

Tasha drags Ellie kicking and screaming into the kitchen and I long for the sound of the microwave.

'Now, you be good for Daddy, alright? He's been under a lot of stress lately and he needs you to go easy on him.'

Tasha has never been able to accept that sometimes I'm actually annoyed at things she does. She just makes out it's my fault because I'm 'stressed'.

'She's five,' I say, through a mouthful of crumbs as I sit down at the table. 'She doesn't know what you're saying. If you want to have a dig, do it to me.'

'Hey, fine. Give him hell, girl,' she says, ruffling Ellie's hair and smiling at me. Ellie's still not happy. I don't blame her. I'm a grown adult and I can't handle being up at this time. As Ellie's wails begin to build, Tasha takes the Rosie Ragdoll down from on top of the kitchen clock and hands it to her. Ellie stops crying immediately.

'I wish you wouldn't keep giving her that, Tash. It's not a toy.'

'Of course it's a toy, Nick. It's a rag doll.'

Tasha will never have it. Ellie loves the Rosie Ragdoll, but I'm not keen on Tasha handing it her way every time she throws a strop. It sits on top of our kitchen clock, looking far too much like a freaky version of the fictional scarecrow Worzel Gummidge for my liking, with bits of glued-on straw poking out of its trousers and sleeves, a straw boater slightly askew on its head. My mum used to have it in her kitchen. We bought it for her shortly after Dad died. One of those stupid 'saw this and thought of you' gifts, but it meant the world to her. Every time Ellie went over she'd want to play with it, even as a small baby. She was fascinated by it. We had to make sure she was careful with it, as it wasn't meant to be a toy – despite what Tasha says.

I don't have a whole lot to remember my mum by, but the Rosie Ragdoll (God knows why she called it that) is one small token that sits up out of the way, looking over us all. Mum died shortly before Ellie's second birthday, from the same cancer that took dad eight years earlier. So to see Tasha casually chucking the Rosie Ragdoll to Ellie like some sort of pacifier or comfort blanket really rankles.

'I just think we should be careful with it,' I say. 'That's all.'

She walks over and kisses me on the top of the head. 'She's fine. She's a good girl. Anyway, it worked, didn't it? Now, you get that coffee down you and stop being such a grumpy puss.'

'What else do you expect, Tash? It's five in the morning. I don't see why we all have to get up just because you've got to go to some bloody conference.'

'Trust me, Nick, it's better than having me worrying all morning about whether you've woken up and actually remembered to take Ellie to school,' she replies, pouring sugar-coated cereal into a bowl for Ellie. Great. Just what an emotionally unstable five-year-old needs at this time of the morning.

'Any idea what time you'll be back?'

'Late. If it finishes on time I should be out of there by six, home by ten with any luck. As long as the trains aren't full of suits.'

I raise my eyebrows momentarily. She'd never have it that she was one of them. Her job was far more important than whatever it was they did for a living, and it always would be.

'Right. Must dash,' she says, grabbing her shoulder bag from the back of the chair and planting a kiss on Ellie's cheek. 'You have a good day at school. Work hard and be good. And you have fun,' she adds as she does a childish little wave to me across the table, her fingers bending and straightening in one unit.

Within seconds she's gone and it's just me and Ellie. Same as it always is.

2

TASHA

Sometimes I think the only reason Nick and I have stayed together is because of Ellie. I hate to say it, but it's probably true. I think it's something I've always known. That's not to say that we had Ellie so that we wouldn't break up, but I think deep down I wondered whether it would change our relationship to have a child. It did, but not in the way I'd expected.

The initial joy was over pretty quickly when I told Nick I wanted to go back to work earlier than planned. Earlier than he'd planned, anyway. He wanted me to take the full twenty weeks, telling me we could make do on the statutory allowance. He's never been one for handling money well, but I would've thought even he'd realise that swapping my salary for a hundred and twenty quid a week wasn't going to cut it. Not with a new child in tow. Not with his income being so unpredictable. If there was one thing I was always sure of, it was that I wanted to be able to provide for my child, to give my child everything she deserved.

We finally agreed on eight weeks, allowing me to keep most of my salary, then going back on the basis that I could work from home two or three days a week. What Nick didn't know at the time was that I'd already told my manager I'd be back part-time after the minimum two weeks and back to full-time after another six. I don't like lying, but Nick's the sort of person you have to lie to occasionally just to make things easier, smooth things over.

When I fell pregnant with Ellie, we'd been trying for years. Over the first couple of years things seemed to be going alright. Work was fairly stale for me, and Nick was still struggling to hawk his first book, but the possibility of having a child was something to cling on to. The dwindling of that possibility seemed to coincide with Nick getting his first book deal and work getting better for me, too, so the thought of having children kind of fell by the wayside.

We'd gone down all sorts of routes and had pretty much come to terms with the fact that nothing was going to happen. I fully expected us to separate within the next few months. I started to take on more responsibilities at work, perhaps partially to distract myself from the toxic atmosphere at home, but mainly because my career had taken off. We'd just taken on a huge new client and I'd been put in charge of managing the project. Three weeks later, I found out I was pregnant.

I was delighted, but at the back of my mind was this constant worry about how I was going to balance a baby and my career. Nick working from home would be a blessing, but I also knew that there was no way he was going to see it like that. He's all about long walks in the country and idealistic family days out. He never thinks about the fact that we somehow have to pay for all that.

He's so derisive and dismissive about my job, it makes me sick sometimes. I think he sees me as one of the faceless hordes of commuters that pass our house every morning on the way to the station. I see them, too, on the train, their faces growing more and more haggard every day. I know I'm not one of them because I feel more and more invigorated with each day, excited about the path my career is taking and how it will enable me to build a future for our whole family. But he doesn't see that. He thinks I'm just doing this for me.

The conference today is a big opportunity. Networking could be vital for building my career further, which would give us more security as a family and give Ellie a better start in life. After all, that's why any of us go to work, isn't it? Because we want the best for our families. But does Nick ever see it like that? Does he hell.

I think he projects. That's Nick's problem. He can't come to terms with the fact that it's his own sense of failure and his own insecurities that are at the root of the problem. He's so fed up with the fact that he's been unable to replicate the success of *Black Tide* that he seems to assume everyone else is a failure too. He's a good dad, though. Mostly. When it doesn't involve him having to be organised. He dotes on Ellie, and she loves him, too. Sometimes I look at her and I imagine that I see confusion in her eyes, almost as if she's unsure as to who I am, as if she sees Nick as the mother figure. I'm sure I'm imagining things, but sometimes I can't help but feel guilty. And then I remember it's just Nick projecting and I refuse to let myself feel like that.

I know I'm not a conventional mother. Perhaps it's my upbringing. My parents aren't as lovey-dovey as Nick's were. But that doesn't mean I love my family any less. He only needs to look at what's in front of him to see my love for Ellie.

All couples have their ups and downs, and I often feel like we mostly have downs, but then I remember Ellie. Our miracle girl. She's the reason I work so hard. She's why I get up at the crack of dawn – and often before it – and come back late at night. I don't get to see her half as often as I'd like to, but that's the sacrifice a parent has to make sometimes. What Nick doesn't see is that I'm doing it for her. For us.

3

NICK

We've got some time to kill. I'm feeling pretty angry with Tasha for having got us up so early. I'm angry because I'm tired, because Ellie needs her sleep at her age and because Tasha's insinuation was that I'm a useless father who can't be trusted to wake up on time and get my own kid to school.

I often tell Tasha that she could spend more time with Ellie by working shorter hours, which would mean not having to get her up hours before she's due at school. It can't be any good for her development, and those long hours certainly aren't working wonders for Tasha, either. She always says we need the money, but I'm pretty sure we don't. We've never been rich, but we've never really had serious money problems, either. Besides which, it's not all about money.

I'm sitting on the sofa, my eyes glazed over as I half-heartedly pretend to enjoy watching the cartoons on the screen. Ellie sits on the carpet in front of me, her legs crossed as she's transfixed by the bright colours and wacky sounds coming from the TV.

I know I'm meant to know the difference between all these kids' shows, but really they're all the same to me. When it comes to kids' TV, it's just a case of bright flashing lights and lots of noise. It's always amazed me how there's so much money in kids' entertainment when really it's just a piece of piss.

I compare this in my mind to the book I'm working on right now. The bastards who write this sort of kids' stuff don't have to worry about plot holes. Just chuck a monster in to explain it all away. Character arcs? Forget it. As long as everyone's throwing gunge at each other, you're golden. Maybe I'm missing a trick. Maybe this is the sort of stuff I should be writing. What's pride when you've got a nice sack of cash to sit on?

I don't think any less of Ellie for it. Of course I don't. She's just like any other five-year-old, sucked in by the whole thing. Part of me would love to give her a more classical upbringing but, if the truth be told, I don't know how. I sometimes wonder if I was ever cut out to be a father. But then I look at Ellie's beaming smile and I realise I wouldn't have it any other way.

I've even suggested to Tasha that she get a different job that would allow her to spend more time with me and Ellie. She looked at me like I'd just dropped down from Mars. I get it. She loves her job. That's great. But I think she enjoys the challenges and the responsibility as opposed to actually having a deep-seated love of marketing renewable-energy products. She doesn't get the irony of her job consisting of singing the praises of a new mode of living, becoming more self-reliant and enjoying the world more – a job that she does from the confines of a stuffy office that she has to spend two hours a day getting to and from.

I look at my watch. It's still only seven thirty. We've got at least an hour before we need to worry about leaving the house. I try to engage Ellie in conversation but she's not interested. Why would she be? I rarely prove to be interesting conversation for adults, never mind a kid.

She's a sweet kid, but she's a child of her time. I sometimes wonder whether she'll end up missing the experience of genuine human connection. As a family, we never just sit down and talk. Most families don't, I guess, but that doesn't mean it's not a problem.

If I'm perfectly honest, I'm quite happy right now just sitting here watching her smile and gawp in amazement. She's perfectly happy. Then again, she doesn't know anything else. This is the world she knows and accepts. She wasn't around to see the change.

I wonder what changes she'll see in her lifetime. Things we can't even comprehend, probably, just the same as our parents couldn't have even imagined the concept of the internet when they were children, and our grandparents couldn't have envisaged the advent of television before it was invented if they'd tried. Whatever the next big technological leap is going to be, it'll be something that we can't even dream up the concept of yet. That's the sort of thing that goes through my mind sometimes, and it tends to give me a bit of a headache.

I've got a headache now, but that's mainly due to the fact that I was dragged from my bed at five o'clock this morning when I could've easily got up later and still been fine. Tasha's not just in our lives – she rules them, too. She has a way of doing that – worming her way in and somehow managing to become indispensable. Sometimes I think she does it by making me feel more and more useless, resulting in me having to rely on her. I know I don't, though. I'm a man. I need to retain that level of independence.

With independence, though, comes responsibility. I'm not foolish enough to think that I'm the most responsible person in the world. I forget things. I'm serially late. I do things in the wrong order. I get my priorities muddled. But no-one's perfect. Tasha's the organised one in our relationship, and that's fine. A relationship with two Tashas in it sure as hell wouldn't work.

This is why I don't like getting up early. My brain's always too active and I end up thinking things like this. I sigh deeply, rest my head back against the sofa and close my eyes.

4

NICK

I jolt awake with a start as Ellie giggles at the TV screen. I'm dazed for a moment, clearly having woken up at the wrong place in my sleep cycle. I blink and look at the clock on the wall. Shit.

What I really don't need right now is another ear bashing from Tasha or the school about how I have a responsibility to get Ellie to school on time. I already know that, but it doesn't help. I'm just not good with responsibilities. Never have been.

I rush to try and get Ellie into her uniform. She hates it, and I'm not keen either. The drab grey fabric looks more like something from a Russian Gulag than a state primary school. Having seen the inside of Hillgrove Primary, the two aren't so different. I remember my days at primary school being full of colour and laughter. Whenever I go inside Ellie's school, it just depresses me.

She squirms as I try to pull the jumper over her head, the same as she does every single weekday. We always have to go through this stupid routine, which makes it ten times harder for me.

'No, I'm too hot,' she yells.

'Well, if you stop wriggling you won't be so warm, will you? Now pack it in and put your jumper on.'

It might as well be Groundhog Day, this tedious and energy-sapping routine reminding me that it's only Monday and there are another four consecutive days of this to come.

I hunt around her room for the various bits she needs for her day at school: PE kit, reading log, her bag of sticks for show-and-tell. The amount of things a five-year-old is asked to take to and from school every day is ridiculous. I'm pretty sure we just used to play in sandpits.

I'm almost buried under the chest of drawers, trying to fish out the missing gym sock, when I hear the doorbell go. I ignore it. Whoever it is can wait. It'll only be Jehovah's Witnesses or someone trying to sell me double glazing.

Five minutes later, bag assembled, I slide Ellie's feet into her school shoes, wiggling and pushing them as I do so. I pick her up and carry her down the stairs to save precious seconds. The post has arrived and is on the mat. Only two bills with red *FINAL REMINDER* warnings this time, which is an improvement on Saturday. I put them on the hall table and make a mental note to pick them up later and pay them.

I usher Ellie through the door and out onto the driveway. There's a light mist in the air, but nothing that won't have cleared within an hour or so. It should be a nice day after that. I might even be able to take my laptop into the garden and get some work done out there. Peace, quiet and some sunshine. Can't ask for much more.

The car bleeps to let me know it's unlocked, and I open the rear door, sit Ellie in the child seat and fasten her seat belt. These child seats are ridiculous. They might be safe, but she looks more like an astronaut getting ready to blast off into space than a five-year-old about to do a ten-mile-an-hour car ride to school. The schoolbag's plonked on the passenger seat and we're ready to go. Just as I'm about to start up the engine, Ellie starts yelling again.

'My picture!'

I sigh. I really, *really* don't need this. 'What picture, sweetheart?' I say, trying to sound as calm and unflustered as possible. I don't want my frustrations to rub off on her. That usually only gets her even more worked up and things tend to escalate from there.

'I did a picture of Miss Williams,' she says, glowering at me in that way she does, knowing she'll get her own way.

'Can't you take it in another day?' I ask, fingering the key in the ignition barrel, knowing we're losing precious seconds here and that Miss Williams would far rather Ellie were at school on time than accompanied by a crayon drawing of her.

'No! I need it!' she says, clearly agitated. I close my eyes, feeling them sting momentarily. I decide to cut my losses.

'Right. Stay there. I'll go and get it,' I say, taking the key out of the ignition barrel and pocketing it. 'Where is it?'

'In the kitchen. Near the toaster.' The look on her face has changed completely now that she knows she's got her own way. She knows exactly which buttons to push. I've no doubt she's going to turn out like her mother – absolutely determined to get her own way in every walk of life, no matter what it takes.

I jog up the driveway to the front door, unlock it and skip into the kitchen. Next to the toaster, propped up against the wooden chopping boards, is a piece of A4 paper with a picture of what might possibly be a human being on it. I don't know. It could also be a dinosaur or a goat. All I know is that my responsible fatherly duty is to say 'Oooh, that's a lovely picture!' whenever she shows me one. Tasha always does a much better job of sounding genuinely impressed than I do. I shake my head, pick the picture up and head back out of the house.

I get back into the car and put the key back in the ignition barrel, holding the picture aloft over my left shoulder as I ask Ellie, 'Is this the one you meant?'

I get no response.

I turn around in my seat.

The car's empty.

5

NICK

It's okay. She's playing. She's playing hide-and-seek. That's all it is.

I tell myself all the lies I can muster as my head darts around on my shoulders, scanning the street for any sign of her. I was only inside for, what, thirty seconds? A minute? She can't have got far.

I get to the end of the drive and turn left, calling her name as I jog along the pavement. A guy on a ladder cleaning a window a few houses up on the other side of the road turns and looks at me.

'Have you seen my daughter?' I shout to him. 'She was here a minute ago.'

He shakes his head and turns back to his dirty window.

I jog back in the direction of the house, then past it, and keep calling Ellie's name. There's nothing.

I'm back up the drive and skirting around the car, looking in the bushes – anywhere I can think of – certain that she can't have reached the end of the road on her own, so she must still be somewhere around the house.

'Ellie, this isn't funny. Come out now,' I bark, trying to convince myself that she's somewhere close by and playing a cruel trick on me. Then the realisation of what went through my head a few moments ago hits me.

She can't have reached the end of the road on her own, so she must still be somewhere around the house.

She can't have reached the end of the road on her own.

On her own.

If she's gone, someone has taken her.

I'm well out of my depth here. I fumble in my trouser pocket and pull out my mobile phone, trying and succeeding the third time to enter my passcode as my hands and fingers tremble.

I hit the green phone icon and my first thought is for what number I should dial. I know I want the police, but should I still dial *999* from a mobile? Isn't there a different number for mobiles? I can't remember what it is. Surely *999* will still work. Or should I be dialling the non-emergency number? I can't remember what that is, either, and as far as I'm concerned this is an emergency. I do the only thing I can and dial *999*.

There's an operator on the end of the line very quickly, and I tell her I want the police. Within a couple of seconds I'm put through, and before I can even think straight I'm babbling garbled words about my daughter having disappeared, someone having taken her and far too much detail about the picture she drew of Miss Williams.

The man on the other end of the phone does his best to calm me down with his matter-of-fact questions.

'How long has she been missing?' he asks.

I glance at my watch. I don't know. It feels like hours, weeks, years, but it can only have been minutes at best. I don't even know what time we got to the car in the first place. Right now, I barely know my own name.

'I don't know. Not long. But she's never done this before. I left her for thirty seconds. I've looked. I don't know.'

I can feel tears breaking.

'And you say you last saw her outside your house? Have you searched the street and spoken to your neighbours to see if they saw anything?'

'I looked. And asked the man on the ladder. I can't find her. She's nowhere. Please just help me. Please come and find her.'

'How old is your daughter?' he asks.

'Five. She's meant to be at school,' I say, my brain switching into organisational – safe – mode. 'She's going to be late.'

'Try not to worry too much,' he says, trying to sound soothing but instead coming across as patronising. 'Most children return very quickly. It's usually just a misunderstanding. Do you have any friends or family around who could help you look?'

'No, I don't. Please, please just come and help me. I . . . I think she's been abducted.'

At the other end of the phone I hear what sounds like either the clicking of a computer mouse or the man's tongue against the roof of his mouth.

'Is there someone who would want to abduct your daughter, sir?'

'I don't . . . I don't know. But I've looked everywhere. She isn't here. There's no way for her to have got in the house. I was there. I've checked the front garden and you can't get into the back from the front. I've looked all around the street. She isn't there!'

'Okay, sir, try not to panic,' he says, riling me even more. 'Could she have reached the end of the street in the time you were apart?'

'No,' I say, firmly. 'No chance. It's impossible.'

There's what could only have been a few seconds' silence, but it seems like hours before he next speaks.

'What I'm going to do is I'm going to send some local officers out to you. In the meantime, can you knock on your neighbours' doors and ask them to check their gardens and houses? It's possible she might have wandered into someone else's property quite innocently.'

'I will,' I tell him. 'Thank you.'

I have to tell Tasha. I tap her name in my 'Favourites' list and the call takes an age to connect.

'What is it, honey? I'm just about to head into the office,' she says, without giving me a chance to speak or even saying hello.

'Ellie's gone,' I say.

'Gone?'

'Yeah. Gone. I went to get something for her and I came back and she was gone. The police are on their way, but—'

'What do you mean? She left the house?'

'No, she was in the car. I went to—'

'You left her in the car?' she says, her voice rising in both volume and pitch.

'For ten seconds. At the most. I just went to grab something. Then I came back and she was gone. I've searched everywhere, and the police—'

'Christ, Nick.'

That's all she can say. Brilliant.

'Are you coming home?' I ask.

'What choice do I have?' she says. 'And I've only just got here. You *knew* I had that meeting with Maxxon today. Why do you always do this to me?' she says and hangs up the phone.

6

TASHA

Fuck, fuck, fuck. That's the only thing I can think right now. Everything's a noisy blur. Part of me is so angry at Nick. All he had to do was get Ellie ready for school and drop her at the gate. Even he could manage that. She's probably just gone for a wander, I tell myself. She's probably somewhere inside the house or in the garden, or she's gone to a friend's house. Children don't get kidnapped. Not really. Not from people like us.

Besides which, I imagine Nick hasn't looked properly. He'll have done what he usually does and just panicked, unable to deal with even the simplest of situations. And now I'm going to miss the conference and I'm going to miss the Maxxon meeting. I might be able to reschedule the meeting, but the conference is going to go on regardless, whether I'm there or not. It's always a juggling act, and it's one I always seem to lose. I sacrificed spending at least a bit of the morning with Ellie in order to make this conference, and now I'm going to miss that, too. She's growing up without me as it is. I'd love to be able to see her off at the school gate in the morning and be there when she comes out in the afternoon, but if I did that we wouldn't have a roof over our heads. I'm losing the present by providing for the future.

I slide my train ticket into the slot on the barrier and it throws it straight back out the top, the red light flashing and bleeping at me. I try again and get the same result. I fight my way back through the crowd of people tutting behind me and make my way over to the man on the gate. He looks thoroughly bored and fed up. I know how he feels.

'My ticket won't let me through,' I say, handing it to him.

'It's a receipt,' he says. 'You need to insert your ticket.'

I clench my teeth. I just want to get home. Now. I look at the ticket. It's definitely a credit card receipt. I go into my purse again and look for the ticket. I can't find it. 'Look, there's been an emergency,' I say. 'My daughter. I've got to get back earlier than I planned. I don't know where my ticket is, but I've got the receipt so you can see I've bought one.'

'Sorry,' the ticket inspector says. 'That doesn't tell me anything. Just shows how much you paid.'

'Exactly. So you can see it's not for just one journey, can't you?'

'Sorry,' he repeats. 'I can't let you through without a valid ticket. You'll have to buy another one from the ticket office.'

I clench my hand around the receipt, which is now a complete waste, scrunch it up and throw it in the man's direction. I know instantly he could probably order me to pick it up or have me ejected from the station – or worse – but I think he can see the frustration and desperation on my face as he calmly bends down and picks it up himself.

A few minutes and sixteen pounds later, I've got my ticket and I make my way back through the barriers – successfully this time – avoiding making eye contact with the man on the gate.

It seems to take an interminable time for the train to arrive, but the clock tells me it's only three minutes. I get on and find a seat, most of them littered with half-read newspapers and coffee cups.

The train seems to be on the go-slow. They always are around here, but the one time I want it to be quicker, it's not happening. If I could get off and run, I would. I glance down at my phone for what must be the twentieth time since I left London. There's no signal. I keep on at Nick to get our contracts changed and to move on to a provider which actually covers our area of the country properly, but I'm not holding my breath. I've got a signal at home and at work, but that's about it. The countryside in between is a no-go area.

I look at my watch. It should be forty minutes or so before I get to my stop, and then I've got to walk home. It might be quicker in a cab, but that depends on traffic. It'll be a complete waste of time anyway. He'll probably have found her by the time I get back, which will mean waiting for another train back into London and missing the conference altogether. Not to mention the extra expense. I just wish for once in his life he could make himself useful and stop making mine even harder than it already is. I'll get home, we'll find her, and my day will be wasted.

It's not long before I realise this isn't me getting annoyed at what I anticipate happening; it's wishful thinking. I *want* it all to be a complete waste of time. I want it all to be Nick's fault. I want him to find her before I get home. Because if none of that happens, that means only one thing: it means our baby is gone.

7

NICK

I do as I was told and jog down the street, searching gardens and knocking on doors, trying to rouse my neighbours' attention. I'm four houses down on our side of the road before anyone answers. I'm now opposite the man on the ladder and he's looking at me strangely again.

An old lady answers the door. She must be in her nineties.

'Hi. I live a few doors down and I'm looking for my daughter. I think she might have run into someone else's garden or house. Have you seen her? A young girl, about this tall,' I say, holding my hand out to my side.

The woman just looks at me. Considering the number of chains and locks she had to take off the door just to open it a moment ago, I'm guessing there's no way Ellie's in here.

'I'll just look in your hedges to see if she's hiding there,' I say. The woman still says nothing.

I turn and look more closely at her front garden. The grass is overgrown and the 'hedges' are mostly weeds and thistles. I move a few clumps aside with my foot and call Ellie's name, but there's nothing.

At the next two houses there's still no answer, but before I can try the next one I hear the sound of a car engine increasing in volume. I look. It's the police. I jog up the road and wave my arms as they round the corner and pull up alongside me.

'Are you here for my daughter?' I ask.

'Mr Connor, is it?' the middle-aged uniformed policeman asks as he gets out of the passenger-side door.

'Yes. Nick Connor. I don't know what you've been told, but she was in the back seat of the car for a few seconds, if that. I went into the house to get something she'd forgotten and I came back and she was gone.'

'Right. Which house is yours?' he asks.

'Down there,' I say. 'Number forty.'

He gestures to his younger counterpart with a flick of the head and they both follow me down the road towards the house.

'Thank you for coming so quickly,' I say, trying to act as normally as possible, a large part of me realising that they'd probably think I was completely overreacting. 'I thought you usually left it a day or two before looking for people.'

'Depends on the circumstances,' the younger officer says. 'With young children it's a bit different. Especially if there's a chance someone else might've taken them.'

The older officer darts a look at him, thinking I won't notice.

'You seem quite calm, Mr Connor,' the younger officer says. 'Does this sort of thing happen often?'

'No, of course not,' I reply. 'I just didn't want to seem like some panicking lunatic, that's all. Inside I'm a wreck. Trust me.'

The older officer nods. 'I'm PC Briers, by the way,' he says. 'This is PC Robinson.'

I nod. 'That's mine, there,' I say as we get closer to the house. 'She was in the back of the car.'

'Was she strapped in? Was the door locked?' PC Briers asks.

'It wasn't locked, no. I was only gone a few seconds. She was strapped in, though.'

'Was it a safety catch at all? Could she have undone it herself?'

'Well, yeah, she could. She has done before. She's five, for Christ's sake. She's always fiddling with everything.'

Briers and Robinson look at each other. I can tell what they're thinking.

'But she's not the sort of kid to just walk off or disappear. She knows about things like this. We talk about it all the time at home, keeping safe and things like that.'

'You say she can't have disappeared on her own, though?' Briers asks. 'Why's that?'

'I dunno,' I say. 'It just doesn't seem possible. There's no way she could've got to the end of the road on her own in the time I was inside.'

'Do you know of anyone who might have wanted to take Ellie?'

I can see the way he's looking at me. We walk up the driveway to the house.

'No. My wife, Tasha, was at work. She's on her way back but it'll take a while as she works in London.'

'That's Ellie's mum?' he asks. The question strikes me as bizarre, but I guess it's reasonable in the modern age.

'Yeah, it is.'

'Did you hear a car outside while you were in the house?' PC Robinson asks, making himself useful for the first time as I let the officers inside.

'I don't think so. I don't remember hearing anything,' I say. 'Anyway, should we not be outside, looking?'

'That'll all be taken care of,' PC Briers says, smiling as he tries to reassure me. 'There are certain procedures we have to follow. PC Robinson and I are here to speak to you and find out a little more about Ellie, perhaps try to ascertain where she might have gone and why.'

I nod silently. In my very British way, I do all I can do in times of tension and put the kettle on.

I feel helpless and useless as I sit quietly sipping my tea. What is the right thing to do? Should I be here giving as much information as I can to the officers in my living room, or should I be out pounding the streets doing all I can to look for Ellie? Both options seem futile, and PCs Briers and Robinson remind me that there are officers out looking for her. They tell me that my efforts are best put to use at home, providing information and waiting for some further news. There's nothing much more we can do, they say, which just makes me feel useless.

I look at the empty photo frame on the side unit, the photo of Ellie that was in it now sitting on PC Robinson's lap. This is what they'll circulate with a description, they say.

'Is there anything else we should know about Ellie?' PC Briers asks.

I want to ask why the police have only sent two lowly PCs, but my guess is that they're hardly likely to ship out the local equivalent of Sherlock Holmes or Columbo when, as far as they're concerned, it's probably just a case of a wandering child who'll be back home in half an hour.

I shake my head silently. 'She's just a . . . normal girl. She likes all the normal things. Playing with her friends, watching TV, making things. None of it makes any sense.' There's a bizarre haze in front of my eyes as I speak, both mentally and physically. My eyes are clouded with tears and my mind with confusion.

8

NICK

The nature of my own unproductive working days really hits home when I see how much these guys manage to pack into a couple of hours. We've had officers searching the home, looking at nearby CCTV and knocking on doors in the area. We've had the car taken away on a low-loader – it's a crime scene, apparently – and now we've got a detective inspector sitting in our living room, summoned to get to the bottom of what's happened before it's even really sunk in for me.

She introduced herself as Jane McKenna. I imagine she's seen by her male counterparts as a bit of a ballbreaker. It seems ridiculous to say that, with all that's going on, but it's my writer's instinct to want to guess what people's personalities are the second I meet them.

'Does Ellie have any brothers or sisters?' she asks – just one in a long line of questions. DC Brennan is sitting in the armchair, a fairly nondescript guy who hasn't said much at all.

'No,' I say. 'She's an only child.' Just saying those words brings back both the painful memories and feelings of elation. The pain at finding out we couldn't have kids and the joy at discovering Tasha was pregnant with Ellie. 'We weren't really even meant to have Ellie,' I say.

McKenna's ears prick up.

'We were told we weren't able to have children. Before Ellie was born, I mean. Tasha has severe endometriosis. The doctors said it had damaged her ovaries. We were told it meant we couldn't have children. We tried IVF through the NHS but it didn't work. It would have cost tens of thousands of pounds to go private, and we didn't have that sort of money. We just kind of came to terms with the fact that that was how things were. Later, we found out that Tasha was pregnant with Ellie.'

'That must have been quite a shock,' McKenna says.

'You can say that again. The doctors were more amazed than anyone. Actually, it made the papers,' I say, walking over to the side unit and rifling through the middle drawer, pulling out a slim ring binder. 'They called her "the miracle baby".'

I hand the ring binder to McKenna and she leafs through the laminated pages within it, scanning the newspaper cuttings. Brennan peers over her shoulder.

'"Defied the laws of nature",' she says, quoting from a headline.

'Yeah. It was quite something. I must admit we weren't massively keen on the publicity, but you know how these things are.'

I see that McKenna's eyes have stopped moving, but she's still staring at the newspaper cuttings.

'You're a writer, aren't you?' she says. 'Urban horror stuff?'

'Yeah, that's me,' I reply, for some reason feeling a little ashamed.

'I've seen your books. *Black Tide*. That was one of yours, wasn't it? Must be a couple of years ago now.'

'Just over five.'

'Not long after this article was written, then,' she says, finally making eye contact with me. 'Good timing, wasn't it? Must have helped push the book a bit.'

I'm really not sure what she's getting at. 'I guess so,' I say. 'Come to think of it, it was Peter, my agent, who spoke to the papers about all this. Said it would be a human interest story or something.'

She nods silently and looks back at the newspaper clippings. I can see Brennan looking up at me from underneath his brow.

'If you're thinking we got pregnant just to promote a bloody book, I wish it was that fucking easy,' I say, feeling the fury rise to the surface. 'We tried for years – *years* – to have a kid. If you think we could just pop one off on a whim, don't you think we would've done?'

'I didn't suggest anything of the sort, Mr Connor,' McKenna says, offering a disarming smile. She glances back at the newspaper clippings and nods.

A uniformed officer knocks on the already-open door to get our attention.

'Sorry to bother you,' he says, holding up a mobile phone in his gloved hand, 'but this was on the side in the kitchen. Is it yours?'

'Yeah,' I say, standing and holding out my hand. 'Thanks.'

'Ah, no, sorry,' he replies, dropping it into a polythene bag. 'We'll have to take it, I'm afraid.'

I look at McKenna for some help.

'Does Ellie have her own mobile phone?' she asks.

'No, of course she doesn't,' I reply. 'She's five years old.'

'Then he's right,' she says. 'It'll need to be checked. There's a possibility she might have tried initiating contact with someone using it. Are there any laptops or computers in the house – anything that Ellie might have used?'

'Well, yeah, of course. I've got a MacBook in my office. Tasha's got a work laptop and tablet but she's got them with her. She's gone to a conference. She's on her way back, but she's taken a train so I don't know how long she'll be. Ellie doesn't really use them, though. She's only five.' I sit for a moment before McKenna's last comment sinks in. 'What do you mean by "initiating contact"?'

McKenna glances sideways at the uniformed officer, who swiftly leaves the room. 'In a surprisingly large majority of cases concerning missing or kidnapped children, we find that the child had a prior relationship with the person who took them. Now, of course we don't know that Ellie has been taken, but we need to ensure we have all the evidence to hand and consider every possibility, especially considering her age.'

It still doesn't quite make sense. 'But why do you need my laptop and mobile phone?'

DI McKenna exhales heavily. 'We'll need to just check she hasn't had any online contact with anyone. It's routine.'

The thought hadn't even crossed my mind. 'Jesus Christ, she's five years old!'

'You'd be surprised,' she replies, keeping her voice much calmer than mine.

I know I need to keep my frustrations to a minimum and keep calm to maximise the chances of finding Ellie quickly.

'Which school does Ellie go to?' McKenna asks. 'Have you called them to check she hasn't gone in by herself?'

The first thought that hits my mind is that I've got officers trawling through my belongings, confiscating my car and mobile phone, and they've not even bothered to check whether Ellie's just at school. 'They called me,' I say. 'To ask why she wasn't in.'

I can see the way McKenna's looking at me and I can tell what she's thinking. She's thinking it's odd that I didn't call the school earlier and that I had to wait for them to phone me. She's right. It is odd.

'Which school does she go to?' she repeats.

'Hillgrove,' I reply.

McKenna's eyes narrow. 'That's quite a way away,' she says. 'You can't be in the catchment area for that one, surely.'

'We aren't,' I reply. 'She was at Parkview for a while but Tasha had a falling out with the head over some behavioural thing of Ellie's. And she won't send her to St Hilda's because it's a faith school.'

McKenna nods. Again, I can tell what she's thinking. *The fussy, interfering mother.*

'Just easier sometimes to go along with these things, isn't it?' I offer.

McKenna just smiles.

9

NICK

I breathe a huge sigh of relief once they've gone back to the station to circulate the photo of Ellie on their system. On more than one occasion while McKenna and Brennan were here I felt like a suspect in my own home, as if what had already happened that morning wasn't bad enough.

I keep running through that moment in my head. All sense of time has been warped by the adrenaline and sheer panic, but I can only have been in the house a minute at the most. She can't have got to the end of the road on her own in that time, which means someone must have taken her. It's the only logical explanation.

In that time, the person who took her must have been nearby. I rack my brains, trying to think what I saw when I put Ellie in the car. Was anyone walking past? Were there any cars parked up? Try as I might, I can't visualise anything. All I can see is the empty car seat.

I look out the living room window and try to jog my memory, but it's no use. My eyes scan past the end of the drive, across the road and up at the front window of number 39 across the road. I see the silhouette of the man who lives there, standing as still as a statue in his front room, his shape outlined by the sun that streams through from the back of his house. A few moments later, he walks away and his figure recedes.

There have been stories and rumours about this guy. Derek, his name is. He must be well into his late eighties by now. He was easily in his sixties when I was at school, when we lived about three-quarters of a mile away from here.

We used to have to walk down Rushmere Road each day to get to school, and Derek would often be seen standing at his front window, just staring out. On the rare occasions that he'd ventured outside, there had been all sorts of stories about what he'd said or done to kids at the school. I'd always assumed they were just silly schoolboy rumours made up about a lonely old guy who lived on his own. I never thought anything more of it.

When we came to look at this house before buying it, the rumours about Derek did cross my mind but only fleetingly. After all, the guy was overwhelmingly likely to be completely harmless, if a little odd, and for all we knew he didn't live there any more anyway. Of course, since then we had come to realise that he did still live there.

Being Derek's neighbour gave us a completely different insight. He was no longer the weird recluse, but the man who always knew everything that was going on in Rushmere Road. He'd been here since the houses were built and this was his domain. Whenever we had a party, we'd invariably get a visit from the local police at some point, saying there'd been a complaint from a neighbour.

We spoke to the neighbours on both sides about this, and both denied complaining and said they'd had the same issues in the past and had suspected Derek. Of course, nothing had ever been done about it by the police as the noise would've been barely audible from the road, let alone Derek's house. He just didn't want to see other people having fun. As far as I'm concerned, living on your own and as you want to is absolutely fine, but don't try to stop other people having fun.

I don't think any of our neighbours have ever had a conversation with Derek. I know I certainly haven't, and I've never seen him talking to anyone else. The only time anyone ever sees him is if they happen to be looking out of their window at eight o'clock in the evening when, regular as clockwork, Derek takes a black bin bag out of the house and puts it in his wheelie bin.

In a roundabout way, he got what he wanted anyway. We haven't had a party in years, and I don't recall any of our neighbours even having had the TV up loud.

A thought occurs to me. With the amount of time Derek spends standing at his front window, he's more likely than anyone to have seen something. His house is right opposite ours, and he can see our whole driveway. Any sign of something going on across the road and he'd be straight at the window with his binoculars out.

Before I've even thought about what I'm going to say, I've slipped my shoes on and I'm out of the door, jogging down the driveway and across the road to number 39. I knock on the door and wait, catching my breath. There's no answer.

I knock again, knowing damn well Derek's in as I've just seen him. I think maybe he's a bit deaf, so I knock louder. He'd better not be deaf, especially not after complaining about the noise so much. After a few moments I sigh and walk back down his drive. As I reach the end, I spin on my heels and catch sight of him disappearing behind a curtain as my eyes meet the window.

I march back up his drive and knock on the window.

'Derek, I just want to speak to you. Please. I've got a problem and I want to know if you saw anything. I need your help.'

Silence. Well, that went well. There's no way I can force this guy to open his door. The best I can do is mention him to the police as a potential witness and hope they don't think I'm losing the plot. They may have spoken to him at some point anyway if they've been going door to door.

As I get back to the end of his driveway and start to look down the road to see if it's safe to cross, I hear the sound of Derek's front door unlatching. I slow and turn around just as it opens. I walk back up the driveway carefully, trying not to seem too anxious or keen. Derek just looks at me, his eyes narrowed, looking both concerned and suspicious at the same time.

'Thank you,' I say, unable to think of anything else. I stand a good fifteen feet away from him, not wanting to get any closer. I consider this an achievement as it is. 'I just need your help. I've lost my daughter. My little girl, Ellie. She disappeared this morning. She was in the car, then I went inside to get something and I came back and she was gone. I wondered if you saw anything. Maybe a strange car, people acting suspiciously. Anything.'

Derek looks at me for a few moments longer, then lowers his eyes to the floor. 'I didn't see anything,' he says, as he takes a step back and closes the door.

10

NICK

I feel completely helpless. There's no other word for it. I can either blindly walk the streets, as I have done for a good half an hour after speaking to Derek, or I can do as the police told me and wait at home in case Ellie returns.

When I get back to the house I sit on a stool at the breakfast bar in the kitchen and rest my head on my arms on the counter. I try to calm my racing mind and think more clearly, trying to remember what I learned from those 'mindfulness' websites. The incredible stress of the whole situation has made my skull feel as though it's been stuffed with cotton wool.

I want to cry, scream, shout and break things all at the same time. I know I'm going to crack, and very soon, but I don't know in which way yet. The next thing I hear is the front door closing and Tasha marching through into the kitchen.

'Oh my god, Nick,' she says, throwing her house keys onto the worktop. 'The trains were held up, something about a signal failure further up the line. I couldn't phone on the way back. I tried, but I had no signal and just as it came back my battery died. I was going to charge it up at work, but—'

She stops speaking as she sees the look on my face. I walk over to her and sob onto her shoulder.

'Where are the police?' she finally asks as I wipe my eyes with the back of my hand.

'They're out looking. They were here a little while ago. Two PCs and a couple of detectives. They wanted to know more about her, what she looked like. I gave them a photo from the living room.'

'What happened? Where could she have gone?' she asks.

I shake my head slowly, clenching my eyes shut. If only I could answer that question. I've tried to answer it myself a hundred and one times already this morning.

'I don't know. I put her in the car, belted her up and then she said she'd forgotten something. A picture of Miss Williams. I told her to forget it and we'd take it in tomorrow, but you know what she gets like. I ran back to the house, grabbed the picture, came back out and she was gone.'

'How long were you in there?' Tasha asks.

'A minute. If that.'

'Oh god, Nick. Why couldn't you have taken her with you?'

I feel slightly as if I'm being accused of something. I know there's no justification for leaving a five-year-old girl on her own, but this still doesn't seem right.

'It was a minute, Tash. Seconds. We were already late for school and I just wanted to get in and out again. Listen,' I say, trying to pacify her but also trying to convince myself. 'The police said she probably isn't far. She might just be hiding in a neighbour's garden somewhere, thinking it's all one big game. You know what kids are like at her age.' I don't mention my suspicions, fast becoming assumptions, that she's been kidnapped.

'Jesus Christ, Nick. How could you be late? You were up at five!'

I've got no response to that.

We sit in the living room and can barely look at each other.

'We should be doing something,' Tasha says. 'We can't just sit here.'

'I know,' I say. 'I feel helpless but there's nothing we can do. We need to wait here in case she comes home.'

Tasha's head darts up and she looks at me. 'What do you mean "*in case*"?'

'I mean in case she comes back to the house on her own before the police find her,' I say, trying not to panic her. Tasha under stress is just about the worst kind of Tasha there is. I need to try and keep things calm for all our sakes.

'Was the car locked?' she asks after a few moments of silence.

'No.'

'Why not?'

'I was gone for a minute at the most,' I say, sighing. I look up at the Rosie Ragdoll. I swear it has sadness in its eyes.

'A lot can happen in a minute, Nick. A lot *did* happen in a minute!' she replies, her voice growing in volume.

'Look, I know it's my fault, alright? It was a fucking stupid thing to do. Don't you think I know that?' I hope the pleading in my eyes is enough to defuse her anger.

Before Tasha can say anything else, the doorbell goes. I go to the front door and answer it. It's McKenna again. I usher her through into the living room, trying to read her face, hoping she has some news.

'Good news first,' she says, fishing my mobile phone out of her pocket. 'You can have this back. They're almost finished with the laptop, too. Another officer will drop that by later.'

I don't even need to ask if there was anything of interest on it. I know there wasn't.

'What about the search?' Tasha asks.

'Our officers are still out looking,' McKenna says. 'There's no sign yet, but that's no bad thing. A five-year-old girl can't get far on her own, like you said, and we got the search started very early so the chances are she hasn't gone far at all. We're still working on the assumption that she's hiding in a neighbour's garden somewhere. You know what kids are like at hiding. We've got officers going door to door along the street, asking your neighbours to check their gardens. But most aren't home this time of day, and obviously we can't get into anyone's back garden without their permission.'

'What do you mean?' Tasha asks, her face showing incredulity. 'Surely if you think she's hiding in someone's garden you need to look in all of them.'

'I'm afraid it's not quite that simple,' McKenna says. 'We're doing what we can. For a start, if she is hiding, we don't want to alarm her by leaping over fences and storming the area. We want her to come out and back home.'

This seems to have pacified Tasha.

'There are a couple of things I need to check with you, though, Mr Connor. I've just been across the road speaking to your neighbour, a Mr Francis?' McKenna's intonation rises on the name, indicating that perhaps I should have a clue as to who this Mr Francis is. She sees the lack of recognition on my face and elaborates. 'At number thirty-nine, directly opposite you.'

'Oh, Derek,' I say. This is the first time I've ever heard his surname.

'His house overlooks yours, so I thought maybe he might have seen something.'

'Yes, that's what I thought,' I reply. McKenna and Tasha both look at me. 'I went over to speak to him. When you left earlier. I wondered if he'd seen any strange cars knocking about or anything like that.'

'Yes, Mr Francis did mention that you visited,' McKenna replies. I try to detect the tone in her voice, but she's kept it as neutral as possible. 'He said he didn't see anything. Nothing out of the ordinary, anyway,' she says. 'I presume he told you the same thing?'

I nod.

'Can you confirm again for me what time you put Ellie in the car, please?' McKenna asks.

'I've already told you this. It was a few minutes before nine.'

'Jesus, Nick,' Tasha says. Trust her to be more worried about Ellie being a few minutes late for school than the fact that she's just disappeared off the face of the earth.

I look at McKenna. 'We were late. I fell asleep,' I say, before turning my glance back to Tasha. 'I'd been up since five.'

'Mr Francis told me he was doing his ironing in his living room, in front of the window, from a quarter to nine until just before quarter past, when we turned up,' McKenna says. 'He would've had a clear view of your driveway, wouldn't he?'

'I guess so,' I say.

McKenna nods, not breaking eye contact with me. 'Not only did Mr Francis say he didn't see anyone odd lurking around, nor Ellie walking off. He says he didn't see you putting Ellie in the car in the first place.'

I see Tasha's head spin round towards me out of the corner of my eye.

'What? No, that's not possible,' I say, but McKenna continues.

'He says the first sign of life he saw was you leaving the house and jogging down the road a few seconds before we got here in the police car.'

'He's lying. He must have seen. He sees everything! How the hell could he miss that? Have you looked at his record?' I say, feeling the beads of sweat breaking on my brow. 'There's something not right about him. How do you know he hasn't got her? There are stories about him.'

'Mr Francis said he thought it was a bit odd,' McKenna continues, 'because you usually set off for school with Ellie sometime between eight fifty and just gone nine.'

Tasha looks at me again. I could really do without her judging me over what time I manage to get Ellie to school, seeing as she's long gone and farting about in London by then.

McKenna stands and paces about the living room as she speaks. 'In fact, he says he went over and knocked at your door a bit earlier this morning. The postman delivered one of your letters to him by mistake, apparently, so he brought it over for you. He says you didn't answer.'

'Well, no. I mean, I heard the doorbell go but I was busy getting Ellie ready for school. It's not exactly easy doing it on your own,' I say, darting a look at Tasha.

'I can imagine,' McKenna says. 'Must be very stressful indeed, day after day. It must eat away at you over time.'

I ignore the comment. 'Anyway, that can't be right,' I say. 'He wouldn't knock or ring the bell. He never knocks on anyone's door. He barely ever answers his own. He would've just put it through the door or stuck it back in the postbox or left it out for the postman the next day. There's no way he would've come and knocked.'

'I've only got your word for that, Mr Connor,' she says. 'Just like I've only got your word for it that you put Ellie in the car when you said you did and that you were in the house when Mr Francis knocked at the door.'

'Well, you've only got Derek's word for it that I didn't, haven't you?' I say. 'Since when is his word taken more seriously than mine?'

McKenna doesn't respond to this.

'Nick,' she says, 'where were you when Ellie went missing?'

11
TASHA

She's only been gone a few hours but it feels like years. There's a bizarre disconnect: some things seem to be moving at a million miles an hour while others drag painfully. My head won't stop spinning. The thoughts are flying through my head as if being fired from a machine gun. The police keep asking questions, confirming things, wanting to know more. What does it matter who her friends are at school? Why do they need to know about extended family? If they'd just get out there and look for her, they'd find her. She can't have gone far.

The pain is indescribable. All that time trying, the failed IVF, being told we would probably never have children. I wonder if that makes it even worse now, knowing that she's missing. We thought it was a miracle when we found out we were pregnant with Ellie. My parents saw her as a gift from God. That's why they chose Grace as her middle name.

I have no idea how to even get through the day. I don't know which way to turn. Even with the police having done their best to be supportive and family and friends rallying round, I still feel completely helpless.

I've always wanted the best for Ellie. What mother wouldn't? You see all these pushy, interfering mothers – the MumsNet Mums, I call them – who are constantly whingeing on Facebook about their child's school or the fact that someone looked at their son in a funny way, instead of actually doing something about it. I've never wanted to be one of those. I need to show her how much I love her. We had a hell of a fight to try and get her into Hillgrove Primary, having been turned down at first. The local education authority wanted to put her in Bolbroke, which is closer to our house and is where Nick went. He was happy with that, but I didn't think it was enough for Ellie. It's my duty as a mother.

Despite the early starts, I've always made the effort to ensure that I see Ellie before I go to work and before she goes to school. It'll do her good. If she gets used to getting up earlier, she'll be more likely to be able to hold down a good job when she's older and be able to provide for her family.

When she's older.

Those words rattle around in my mind, laden with meaning and unsaid connotations that wouldn't have been there a few hours ago. When she was sat at the kitchen table, happily eating her breakfast, looking forward to another day at school. What if she never gets older? What if something dreadful has happened to her?

I can't let those thoughts win out. Nick's convinced that she's been taken by someone. He reckons there simply wasn't enough time for her to get out of her car seat, open the door, close it again and somehow manage to get out of sight and past the end of the road by the time he got back. He says he was in the house for only a few seconds. But I know Nick. Those 'few seconds' could easily have been a minute or more. Two, perhaps. Maybe she did get out of the car and decide to go off exploring. She's five. Kids do that, don't they? Maybe she tried to find her way to a friend's house but got lost. Maybe some Good

Samaritan has taken her in and is trying to get her to tell them where she lives. But wouldn't they have phoned the police by now? Wouldn't the police have put two and two together?

Wherever she is, I just pray to God that she's safe. My parents have always been pretty religious, but fortunately none of that ever rubbed off on me. Now, though, I'm starting to wonder whether prayer might not be a bad idea. What have I got to lose?

The Lord giveth and the Lord taketh away.

Although I'm not one for faith or religion in the slightest, I find myself wanting to pray – to, whatever, call it nature – that Ellie is safe. That she hasn't come to any harm. That she hasn't been taken by anyone who's going to hurt her.

You see it all the time on the TV. Children snatched, predatory paedophiles, missing kids. It all blurs into that distant, removed aspect of life known as 'the news'. It isn't real. Sure, we all watch the cases and have sympathy with them and we all say 'Oh, can you imagine if that happened to us?' but who could? Who could actually know what it feels like to suddenly not have your daughter there any more? I always thought I could, but now I know I couldn't. Nothing could have prepared me for this.

Wherever she is, I just hope she's not suffering. By extension, that means she's either absolutely fine and just wandered off somewhere or . . .

The thought isn't one I can contemplate, and I'm hanging on to every last shred of hope and optimism I have, but they're vanishing fast. I feel so desperate, so completely exposed. I want to scream and make it all go away. I want it to be me that's missing, me that's in danger. Anyone but her. Anyone but Ellie.

12

NICK

It's late. The last few hours have been a blur. It's now starting to get dark and we've still heard nothing.

They've returned my laptop, which is something. Apparently these days it's often just a case of mirroring the machine and then giving the original back.

The accusatory tone of McKenna and the things she insinuated have poisoned the atmosphere in the house, and Tasha's gone out to join the search for Ellie. One of us needed to – it's a case of getting as many people involved as possible – but we also need to keep someone in the house in case Ellie comes back. Tasha made it perfectly clear that person should be me, suggesting that I'd done enough damage today already.

Tasha's put out a Facebook appeal which has already been shared over five hundred times. The police say that if we haven't found her by tomorrow they'll go to the press. Bearing in mind Ellie's age, they say, it's vital that we get the usual appeals out much faster than would otherwise be the case.

It feels like everyone's getting involved. A few of Tasha's former school friends – Emma, Leanne and Cristina – have been in touch. I was surprised at that as she seems to have alienated most of her old friends by setting her sights so blindly on career progression. Tasha's parents are on standby and have planned to fly over from Brisbane on the next available flight if Ellie hasn't been found by tomorrow. I told them that wouldn't be necessary and that by the time they get here we will more than likely have found her anyway.

The last thing I need is them around. Don't get me wrong, we haven't had any major fallings out, but I really couldn't cope with them right now. I know they'd be putting the blame on me, telling me what they would have done differently, how they never let Tasha – who they only ever call Natasha – out of their sight when she was younger. It feels like they use every possible opportunity they have to make me feel small. They denigrate my work and look down on what I do as somehow inferior and not a 'proper job'. What I need right now is support, not people to make me feel worse.

Julie and Tim are good people, but I can't deny that it's a relief knowing they're on the other side of the world. Life has been so much quieter and easier since they moved away. My parents, on the other hand, would have known just what to do. Mum would have gone straight into organisational mode, drawing up maps and itineraries and splitting everyone off into groups. Dad would do his best at keeping everyone calm and spirits high. I've missed that direction and positivity since they died.

It's impossible to describe what it feels like to be in the position where you know you need to do everything but can't possibly do anything. Lying in your bedroom staring at the ceiling while everyone you know is out looking for your missing five-year-old daughter feels so wrong on every conceivable level, but there really is no other option.

You always hear people say that the worst part is the not knowing. I've never really understood that phrase until now. Not knowing where she is. Not knowing whether she's coming back. Not knowing if she's with anyone. Not knowing if she's safe. Not knowing if she's happy. Not knowing if she's alive.

Not knowing.

I guess it's one of those moments when your life changes forever. There was before Ellie disappeared and after Ellie disappeared. A firm, deep line in the sand. A gulley. A canyon. Not to be crossed. My new life began on this day.

I ponder this and many other things, but nothing seems to help. There's nothing that will bring Ellie back other than looking for her and I can't even do that. All I can do is lie here and feel shit and sorry for myself. Because it's my fault. I was the one who left her in that car. Tasha's right. She's always right. If I'd just taken her back inside with me, or even manned the fuck up and told her she could take the picture in tomorrow, we'd all be sitting around the dinner table right now talking about our days. As it is, I haven't eaten since breakfast, the dining room's in darkness and Miss Williams still hasn't got her picture.

I'm not too bad with technology, but it does get in the way of real life sometimes. The text messages and phone calls are endless, with friends and family phoning one after another. I appreciate their support and want to get the word out about Ellie as much as we possibly can, but no-one's come round to the house. No-one actually wants to do anything more than fire off a quick pseudo-supportive text. The most depressing fact is that most of them probably found out through Facebook.

I've become quite adept at cancelling the calls that come through from numbers I recognise. I've changed my voicemail message to say that I'm passing calls from friends and family to voicemail as I need to keep the line free in case the police call. This is partially true, but I also don't want to speak to anyone right now.

A few have taken to emailing me instead. My iPhone's email icon has a red blob telling me I've got nineteen unread emails. I can't cope.

I can't keep up. Messages of support are all well and good, but the only message I want is one that tells me Ellie has been found safe and well and is on her way home.

As I'm looking at it, the phone pings like a hotel reception bell and the number changes to twenty. The alert message at the top of the screen shows that the new email's subject line is *Ellie*, but the name is one I don't recognise: Jen Hood.

Must be another friend of Tasha's, I think, but then why would she be emailing me? I haven't opened any of the other emails, but then I know who they're from and I can almost guess word for word what they're going to say.

There's no way in hell I could have guessed what this email from Jen Hood says, though. I open it and read it three times, just to be sure my mind isn't playing tricks on me.

> *ELLIE IS SAFE. YOU CAN HAVE HER BACK AFTER YOU KILL YOUR WIFE.*

13

NICK

I must have read that email a hundred times over the past few minutes. I've stared at every word, every letter, willing them to say something different. I've looked for the deliberate joke, the typo, the sign that it might have been sent to the wrong person.

Perhaps it's been sent to the right person, but it's just a bad joke. I'm sure I heard somewhere that this happens in cases like this. Troublemakers – trolls, they call them – like to prey on people when they're at their lowest ebb.

I look for signs of some sort of mistake. There's nothing. Maybe this really is an email from someone who wants me to kill my wife to get my daughter back. But why? What the hell can Tasha have done for someone to want her dead? It makes no sense.

Is there some ex-lover I don't know about? Someone she's shafted at work? Both are perfectly plausible in Tasha's case, but she tends to upset people through her self-centred ignorance as opposed to any sort of deliberate malice. For someone to want her dead, she has to have done something pretty serious. But if someone wanted her dead that much, why not do it themselves? Is this some way of getting at me? In order for any of this to make any sense, I need to find out who this person is.

I march into my office and flip the lid up on my MacBook. Fortunately, it starts up about ten seconds after I press the power button, and twenty seconds after that I'm staring at the Facebook login screen.

I've only ever used Facebook about five times in my life, so I struggle to remember my username and password, but I'm lucky on the third attempt and I'm greeted by a newsfeed showing me pictures of my own daughter, shared by family and friends from around the country. I try not to look at the photos and instead click the 'Search' bar at the top of the page and type in *Jen Hood.*

There are so many results, I don't know where to start. There are Jens, Jennys and Jennifers. There are women with Hood as their married name and some with it listed as their maiden name. There are even some Jens who live in towns called Hood or work for companies or went to schools called Hood. Most are from America, but there are a couple in Scotland, Ireland and even France.

None of them are friends with Tasha, or even have any mutual friends with me whatsoever. This person is a complete stranger.

I pick up my phone and go to start calling the police. But I stop. I need to get things into perspective. There are some fucking sick people in the world. People who prey on the families of victims, trying to wind them up. Trolls. Finding my email address online probably isn't difficult, so someone's clearly found it and decided to try and get kicks out of our despair. If that's what this is, do I really want to have the police wasting time tracking down a fifteen-year-old keyboard warrior instead of finding the person who kidnapped my daughter?

I need to make a judgement call. I'm ninety-five percent certain that this is some sick bastard trying to wind us up. And if that's the case, I want to mete out my own brand of justice. Never mind a caution from the police; people like this deserve to feel exactly how they make their targets feel. For that, though, I need to play along and get closer to this Jen Hood person.

I look back at Facebook. Where do I start? I can't just send them all messages saying *Did you kidnap my daughter?* I grab my phone and look at the email again. It's come from a Gmail address: jenhood999@gmail.com. No clues whatsoever as to where the person lives.

Once again, that same feeling hits me: the feeling of not knowing. Someone has sent me this email and I don't have a clue who it could be. Is Jen Hood even her real name? Could she be one of the women staring out at me from my MacBook screen right now? If so, who? Does she actually have Ellie or is this some sort of cruel trick?

No. I'm still sure it's a trick. I remember from reading some crime thrillers that a problem police often have is weeding out the cranks from the real information and clues they get. There's a whole subsection of society that gets its kicks from trying to interfere in police investigations and sending idiotic letters and messages claiming to be responsible. It's all part of the desire to be seen as powerful and in control. It's a psychological disorder, and a dangerous one, too.

I vaguely recall reading about the investigation into the Yorkshire Ripper in the seventies. After ten women had died, the police received letters and phone calls from someone with a Wearside accent claiming he was the Ripper. The police took it seriously and focused their search on Wearside. In the meantime, the real Yorkshire Ripper carried on and killed three more women.

In a way, I hope that's what this is. It would be the sickest possible prank to play, but at least it would mean that its contents weren't real. Though, as much as I try to deny it, something about the message seems all too real. I don't know if it's a sixth sense or what, but I can almost feel the sincerity and determination behind those words. But that leads me to one enormous question: Why?

Tasha's not the most likeable person in the world, but I can't see anyone actively wanting her dead. She's not purposely vindictive. She's just . . . clueless. She only thinks of herself. I rack my brains, trying to think of a time she might have done or said something that would make someone want to kill her. If she did, the person would have to be completely mentally unhinged to make that sort of leap. You hear about it all the time, though, don't you? Psychopaths who take one word the wrong way, or think someone is the devil incarnate. They think they're doing the world a favour. Is that what this is? Or does Tasha have some huge secret in her past that I don't know about? I doubt it, but right now I can't discount the possibility.

Presuming it is real, what can I do? Sure, I can go to the police with it, but then it'd either be taken seriously or treated as a potential hoax. If it's the former, what can they do? Odds are it will have been sent from an internet café or some sort of anonymous server. And if they're just going to treat it as a hoax, I can do that myself. Overall, though, I don't want to take any police resources away from finding Ellie. Deep down, I know that there's another reason why I don't want to alert the police to the email just yet, but that's not something I'm willing to entertain.

No. I need to find out more about this person, lead them into a trap and discover who the hell thinks this sort of shit is funny. And if it's something I'm going to need to go to the police about, I need more information first. I need to make sure this isn't a hoax.

I do the only thing I can do. I hit 'Reply' and start typing.

I delete my words so many times, I can't even remember what I've written before. By the time I've finished it's boiled down to just three words, which I look at again before pressing 'Send'.

Who are you?

14

TASHA

I've been up all night worrying. I knew I would be. The warning signs are all there from before: the breathlessness, the constant dark thoughts, the unshakeable desire to hide away from it all.

There's nothing I can do. Nothing. It's self-perpetuating. My cognitive behavioural therapist reckoned it was to do with a perceived lack of control. He taught me to try to accept that some things are out of my control. And I can, to an extent. I no longer get anxious in traffic jams and I don't flip out so much when my computer crashes. But there's no way I can just let this go. Not knowing where Ellie is, whether she's safe. Knowing that I *could* have been in control. I could have not gone to that conference. I could have stayed at home and been there.

The last time I felt so completely desolate was about a year before Ellie was born. We'd tried conceiving naturally, we'd tried IVF and we were left with nothing. I can't describe what that felt like. To know I'd probably never carry my own child was devastating. Most women take it for granted. Many spend their young adult lives trying to avoid it. But for me, my whole life ended when I found out that I couldn't have a child of my own. It was yet another thing I couldn't control. Something I couldn't predict or influence.

It's the only time in my life I've taken more than a day or two off work. I couldn't face the world. I couldn't even open my front door. My friend Emma recommended that I see one of the GPs at the practice where she works. Nick and I had been seeing a GP there for a little while with regards to the IVF and trouble conceiving, but after the failed IVF Emma recommended we see Dr Mirza. Working on reception, Emma was able to ensure we could get an appointment that suited us and she confided in us that Dr Mirza had had a similar history herself, which might make her the ideal doctor to speak to.

I can still remember walking into the waiting room that afternoon, which is bizarre as everything else from that time feels like an indistinct blur – images crossing over and merging into one another, nothing clear or distinct. I remember Emma's professionalism as she marked me in and told me to sit down in the waiting area. I remember the benevolent smile on Dr Mirza's face as she welcomed me into her room and sat me down beside her desk. And I remember it all coming out, a jumble of words, thoughts and feelings, watching Dr Mirza's brow furrowing as she smiled and nodded – a gesture she'd no doubt practised a thousand times before.

She recommended counselling, told me they worked in partnership with a very good service that helped couples who were struggling to deal with being unable to have children. She told us we could adopt – every bloody person we spoke to told us we could adopt, as if it had never crossed our minds. I told her we didn't want to adopt. I told her I didn't want to speak to any counsellors. I didn't want to speak to anyone full stop. I wanted to hide and forget.

She prescribed me fluoxetine and temazepam. The temazepam was to help me sleep, and I later discovered that fluoxetine is better known as Prozac. I still remember the words she used, though. She said it was *an SSRI, to take the edge off of things*. At the time, I didn't care. Most of me wanted to curl up and die, and another part just wished everything would go away. Taking the edge off would be a good start. I was back at work not long after, the medication helping me to at least function. That was all it did do, though. I certainly didn't feel happy. I didn't feel anything much. And then four months later I discovered I was pregnant. Eighteen weeks and three days later, to be precise. I took five tests – a second one straight away, and then three on each consecutive day thereafter. I had to be sure. We'd waited so long.

I took my last dose of fluoxetine a few hours before that first positive pregnancy test. I'd been cycling on and off of temazepam as and when it was needed, and that also stopped the moment I knew I was pregnant. I was going to do nothing to put this baby's life at risk. I didn't need chemical stimulation to get me through the day. Excitement and pregnancy hormones more than got me through.

Last night, I contacted Emma. She said she would book me an appointment to see Dr Mirza, but that she was out on house calls in the morning. I told Emma a house call would be best – I need to stay at home in case Ellie comes back. Even the thought of leaving the house at the moment frightens me. Sitting in a waiting room full of people, watching the clock tick by, is completely unthinkable.

I jump as I hear the car door close and I get up to look out of the window. I see Dr Mirza walking up the driveway. I go to the door to meet her, and ask her to come through to the living room. As soon as she asks me what the problem is, I break down and it all comes out. A long, rambling string of words that don't even make any sense. It's like history being repeated all over again, Dr Mirza's brow furrowing as my eyes mist over with tears, not even hearing my own words.

She asks me how long Ellie's been missing, what the police are doing, how Nick's coping with it all. I answer all of her questions as best as I can. The fact of the matter is that everything is blurred. My whole concept of time is gone. I don't know what the police are doing. I don't know how Nick's coping with it all. These are all things I should know.

I'm super-organised, super-efficient, a supermum. And today I'm far from being any of those three things. For all I know, I might not even be a mum any more.

This thought has me panicking, my heart racing as I start to hyperventilate. Dr Mirza tries her best to calm me down. 'I know there's nothing you can do, but I can't sleep,' I tell her. 'I can't think straight, I can't eat. I can't function.'

She prescribes me diazepam and tells me a district nurse will be round later to deliver my prescription. Even in the state of mind I'm in now, I know this isn't something they usually do. Doctors are very pushed for time and can't always do home visits, never mind get medication delivered to you the same day. I can't help but think that perhaps Dr Mirza's own past experiences might have influenced her decision. I don't make out that I know anything – I never have – and I tell her I'm incredibly grateful to her. This sets me off again. I try to steady myself, knowing that the medication will start to take the edge off of things. Knowing that there's someone there to help me get through this. After all, the one person I should be able to rely on seems to be falling apart himself.

15

NICK

I barely slept a wink throughout the night, and the worrying got even worse. Ellie's been missing for almost twenty-four hours now, but it feels like so much longer. Once Tasha had come home and the police had called off the search for the night, the sheer panic reached its apex.

Not only was she still missing with no-one out looking for her, but it was dark and cold and we had no idea where she was or if she was safe. Bizarrely, the only thing that kept me vaguely sane was the ransom note I'd had earlier in the evening. At least if I convinced myself it was genuine then it meant Ellie was alive and safe. The fact that I've not had a response yet is starting to worry me, though.

We had all the usual lines from the police. *The vast majority of missing people return home safe and sound within forty-eight hours, if not twenty-four.* If I had a pound for every time I'd heard that since yesterday, I'd be a millionaire.

We've had an officer camped out on our doorstep all night. We're not quite sure why. The official police line is that they want to protect us from any undue media attention. In my paranoid state, I'm convinced they want to keep an eye on us. I've read enough crime books to know that close family are always the first to come under suspicion. Statistically speaking, they're the most likely to be guilty.

The local BBC radio stations are running the story on their news bulletins, and Tasha's Facebook status has been shared almost a thousand times. There are huge great posters of Ellie being put up around the neighbourhood. It's both comforting and oddly disconcerting. By now, everyone in the town and the area is more than aware of Ellie and still no-one has seen her. That's both a worry and a reassurance, in that it means she's probably not in the area and that she's probably with someone. Again, it's the not knowing *who* that's the problem.

Tasha's downstairs on the phone to her parents, and the police are out doing their door-to-door enquiries while I sit here on the bed, not knowing what to do. That's the worst part of it.

My phone vibrates on the bedside table and my heart stops as I see the words on the notification.

Jen Hood

Re: Ellie

I unlock my phone and jab the email icon. It seems to take an age to load, but I finally open the email and read the message.

Hope young copper stood outside your house isn't there for 'protection'.

You know what happens if I find out you told them.

I'm looking at Ellie right now. I've got eyes on you too. Say one word to the police and I will kill her immediately.

Only one way you can get her back.

The staccato sentences worry me. They sound like someone panicked. If this person has Ellie, the last thing I want them to do is panic. I fire off a reply as quickly as I can.

I told no-one. I understand.

I hope this says it all while remaining deliberately ambiguous. The possibility is still there at the back of my mind that I'm either going to have to go to the police about this person or that it's some sick prank and that they're going to try and lead me into doing something stupid and then call the police themselves. I'm certainly not going to put anything incriminating in black and white.

As I have with the other messages, I make sure I delete both Jen Hood's emails and my replies, both from their main folders and from my 'Deleted Items' folder, too. The police might want to look through my phone and laptop again at some point, and I can't be too careful. I'm sure there'd still be some deeper trace somewhere if they wanted to find it, but there's no reason for them to look more deeply unless I'm actually under suspicion, so I need to make sure that doesn't happen.

As I hit the last 'Delete' button, I jump up and dart over to the bedroom window with the sudden realisation that the person who sent the email must be able to see the house. If they know there's a young policeman standing outside, they must be nearby.

My heart's racing nineteen to the dozen as I try to get my head round this. That policeman's been there since they called off the search last night, so there's nothing to say that this Jen Hood is outside right now. In fact, it'd be pretty stupid for them to be outside right now. But how did they manage to get close enough to the house to see the policeman without him seeing them?

In my mind, there's only one answer to that. They didn't have to go anywhere. They live on the street.

I try to gauge the lines of sight from the other houses on the street to where the policeman is standing. To the right the line of sight would be broken by the huge hedge that separates our house from next door. To the left, whoever was watching would be hidden by the bend in the road on one side and their own walls and hedges on the other. I guess it's feasible that a few houses could have decent sight lines from their upstairs windows, but there's only one which has a perfect view. The house that's sitting there looking at me right now, gloating. Number 39.

I feel the anger flooding into me, thinking back to when Derek told the police he didn't see me putting Ellie in the car. Why would he lie? All I know is that he has to be involved somehow. Why else would he try to throw the police off the scent?

Before I can even reason with myself, I'm bounding down the stairs and out the front door. The policeman turns and looks at me.

'Ah, I was hoping you'd be up soon,' he says. 'Mind if I use your loo?'

'Be my guest,' I say, as I walk quickly past him and cross the road.

Within seconds I'm hammering on Derek's door. He can't have seen me coming, because he opens it shortly after and seems genuinely shocked to see me. I don't wait to be invited in and I make my way through into his kitchen.

He closes the door behind him and shuffles through after me, looking more scared than angry that I've just barged my way into his house.

'Where is it?' I ask, staring him down.

'Where's what?'

'Come on, don't play stupid. Where's your computer?'

'I don't own a computer,' he says, looking confused. 'What the hell would I want with one of those?'

I realise this is the most I've ever heard him say in twenty-odd years of walking past his house twice a day and then living opposite.

'This Jen Hood thing. The emails. What's it all about?' A small part of me appears to be floating above my body, watching ashamedly as my rage and emotion all boils to the surface. The rest of me is completely consumed by it, feeling the blood pulsing in my temples as I stand face-to-face with the man I think has kidnapped my daughter.

It all makes sense. The way he managed to see her, grab her and get her out of sight within the space of a minute and without me hearing a car. The way he knew there was a policeman standing outside my house. It's because he was there all along, right opposite, watching me.

'*Where is she?*' I yell as I start to pace through the archway into his living room before skirting back round and heading upstairs. 'Ellie? *Ellie!*'

The upstairs rooms are filled with rubbish – old ornaments and boxes of papers. I know one thing for certain – there's definitely no computer in this house. The guy doesn't even look as if he knows how to work a vacuum cleaner.

Despite this, I find myself rifling through his belongings, emptying drawers and throwing things all over the place in my desperate search for something – *something* – that might lead me towards Ellie.

I'm back out on the landing and yanking at the loft hatch when I hear the now-familiar voice of Derek downstairs.

'He's up there,' he says.

Before I can get any further, the policeman who'd been standing outside my house is tugging on my arm and leading me back down the stairs.

16

NICK

By the time I've been frogmarched back to my own house by the policeman, McKenna and Brennan are already sitting in my living room, waiting for me. Tasha's there, too.

'What the hell, Nick?' she says, as I try to avoid looking anyone in the eye. The anger has subsided now and all I feel is shame and embarrassment.

'Don't, Tash,' I say. McKenna and Brennan have left the room to speak to the officer who was posted outside and who came to get me out of Derek's house.

'No, seriously, what the hell? We've been out knocking on doors, handing out photos of Ellie, scouring every fucking inch of the area and you're, what, ransacking some old guy's house?'

'Tash, I know. But you have to just believe me, alright? I want Ellie back as much as you do. More than you do.'

'More than I do? Are you serious?'

'It's my fault she went missing, isn't it?' I say, looking at her for the first time. 'Don't you think I don't know that? Don't you think I'm not beating myself up every minute, every second? I want her back, too, and I'm doing what I can, in my own way, to make sure that happens. You just have to trust me, Tash.'

'Trust you?' she says, making a snorting noise. 'Nick, I couldn't even trust you to get her to fucking school.'

There's a few moments of silence before I speak again. 'That's low.'

'It's honest,' she replies. 'What were you doing over there anyway? What did you seriously expect to find? Ellie locked up in a cupboard in his spare bedroom?'

'I thought he might know something,' I reply, knowing I can't say anything more. Not now.

'Like what?' McKenna asks, having re-entered the room silently with Brennan.

'I don't know. I just thought . . . He must have seen something.'

McKenna sighs and shares a look with Tasha before speaking to me. 'We've spoken to Mr Francis again and he confirmed that he didn't see anything. Among other things that he told us,' she adds, leaving the comment hanging in the air like a bad smell.

After a few moments, Tasha offers them tea and McKenna follows her out to the kitchen. I notice they don't ask me if I want anything.

'What were you looking for, Nick?' Brennan asks once they're gone.

'Nothing,' I reply.

'You must've been looking for something,' he says, sitting down in the armchair in what seems like some sort of attempt to lighten the atmosphere. 'I mean, you don't just go around ransacking your neighbours' houses just for the sake of it, do you?'

I'm not sure how to respond to this. What can I say? *I received a ransom email saying I could have Ellie back if I kill Tasha, and I thought he sent it*? Sure, I could very well say that. Only I don't want to. And deep down I know why I don't want to. But I still can't shake the two enormous questions hanging over my head: who and why?

A lot of what's being said to me right now isn't really entering my brain. Their words are sort of floating around the outside of my head, trying to find a way in but not succeeding. All I can think of is that email and why someone would want to send it. I hope to God it's not real, but what if it is? What if this person really does have Ellie and really does want Tasha dead?

An ex-boyfriend? Someone she got into trouble at work? A colleague she screwed over? Some sort of dark shadow from her past who's been waiting, lurking, ready to exact their revenge at the right moment? None of this makes any sense whatsoever.

It's at this point that I realise why my frustrations are aimed at the police investigation and the search for Ellie. It's because I know that the longer the search goes on, the less likely it becomes that Ellie will be found. Most missing children are found within a few hours. After that, it becomes exponentially less likely that they'll be found. If that happens, I'll only be left with one way to get her back. By telling the police about the email I received from Jen Hood, it could potentially help them find her sooner. If it's real. But if it's just a vicious troll? Diverting police resources away from finding Ellie and towards tracking down a troll is the last thing I want. I need to weigh up the odds. Is it more likely this email is real or fake? Right now, there's only one answer to that: the chances are it's a hoax. In these precious first few hours, I desperately need the police to be putting everything into looking for Ellie.

'Let me level with you, Nick,' Brennan says, clearly attempting to play good cop to McKenna's bad. 'I know you're under a lot of stress with the situation. Trust me, I see it all the time. I don't mean that to sound patronising. And I know people respond in different ways to stress. But the way you're behaving and reacting to things . . . Well, it's not doing you any favours, put it that way.'

'What are you trying to say?' I ask, partly grateful for his efforts to see things from my point of view and partly sceptical of his motives.

'I've been doing this long enough to get an eye for a situation. I've got a pretty good copper's nose. I know you didn't do anything to harm Ellie, but the way you've been reacting to things, other people might think otherwise. See what I'm saying?'

I barely hear a word that comes out of his mouth after he says Ellie's name. Even though, thanks to Derek, I know the police have suspected something about me, I'm still stunned by the first actual mention of the possibility that this could have been some sort of deliberate ploy on my part. I can see why it's crossed their minds; you see it all the time in books and on TV, the parents being unhinged and harming their own children and then reporting them missing. The police have to consider everything. But the first time you hear that said about yourself, it's like a ton of bricks landing on your head.

Brennan must have noticed me standing there open-mouthed as he tries to backtrack. 'I'm just anticipating how these things go, you know? Just trying to give you a bit of friendly advice. I'm pretty certain you'll want to make sure we're putting our efforts into finding Ellie and not worrying about what you're going to do next. See what I mean?'

'Yeah. Course.'

'Only, according to Mr Francis, you said something about a computer. You were shouting out Ellie's name and asking him something about an email. What was that all about?'

Now's my chance. I could tell them about the emails and have them put a couple of officers on to finding out who sent them. But I know that's pointless. They'll have been sent in some sort of untraceable way, I'm sure. It's not my area of expertise, but I can only assume the sender will have used some sort of encryption or something. And in any case, who are they going to find? Some kid fucking about on the internet. But almost certainly not Ellie.

I can't deny it, though. The possibility that this is all real and that this Jen Hood person really does have Ellie is growing all the time. Especially since I found out that the person who sent it can clearly see my house. Or can they? Isn't there a bloody good chance that there'd be a police officer outside my house at the moment? Was it just a lucky guess? Or was there some sort of local news coverage which showed the officer in the background?

With the increasing possibility that this is all absolutely real, I feel my entire body flooding with fear. I know this is now or never. But something is still holding me back. Since the incident with Derek lying to the detectives and them suspecting that I've got something to do with it, how can I have any faith in the police? Would they turn this back on me somehow? They seem to have done fuck all so far, and I'm not convinced I can trust them.

My head's spinning. I don't trust the police, but I don't want to use up their resources. I think the messages are fake, but I think they're real. Everything has become a blur and I just want to scream and yell and let it all out and let someone else shoulder the burden, let someone else find her. But I know that isn't going to happen. I've been through enough to know that there's only one person I can trust. One person who I know will do everything within their power to get Ellie back. And that's me.

'I dunno,' I say. 'I've not been sleeping well. I'd been napping and I woke up confused. Lack of sleep does that to me sometimes and it's not exactly easy to let your mind wind down when your five-year-old daughter's missing.'

'Perhaps you should see a doctor,' he says.

'Perhaps,' I reply.

The atmosphere is broken by the return of Tasha and McKenna, clutching their mugs and passing one to Brennan. It still doesn't dawn on anyone that I've not been asked if I want anything. Or perhaps it does and it's a deliberate ploy. The way my mind's working right now, anything's possible.

'Now, Nick, are you going to tell us what that was all about?' McKenna says, getting straight to the point as always. I've got a million thoughts going through my head right now, but the one that concerns me is that they seem to be more preoccupied with me and my actions than they are with finding Ellie.

'Does it really matter? We should be out looking, not going over stuff which doesn't matter,' I say.

'It does matter, though, Nick. It matters that you forced your way into an elderly man's house and ransacked it,' McKenna replies.

'I didn't force my way in.'

'You weren't invited,' she says.

I just shake my head and release a slight smile and a laugh.

'Something funny?'

'Only the fact that we're wasting time here,' I say. 'Anyway, have you looked more carefully at Derek Francis? Everyone around here knows he's not quite right. You'd do better to be questioning him than me.'

'Questioning him about what?' Brennan asks.

'I don't know,' I say, eventually.

McKenna paces towards the front window. 'About Ellie's disappearance, you mean?'

'Why not? He had a full view of the driveway. He's the only one who did. And he says he was stood at the window at the time Ellie went missing. Yet he still didn't see anything. That's a bit weird, don't you think?'

'Not particularly. It comes down to your word against his, doesn't it? You say you put Ellie in the car and went back inside. Derek Francis says he didn't see you do anything of the sort. He also says he rang your doorbell earlier that morning to give you the letter he'd had delivered to his house by mistake and got no answer.'

'I've already told you all this,' I say, frustrated. 'I didn't answer because I was getting Ellie dressed. And I doubt very much it was him at my door, seeing as he doesn't communicate with anyone. He's a hermit.'

'Was the letter on your mat when you came downstairs?' McKenna asks.

'Well, yes.'

She just looks at me. 'So it would seem that that part of his story is true. Why not the rest?'

'Because he's lying. I know exactly what happened that morning. I was there. I'm not some senile old pensioner who doesn't know what he sees and doesn't see.'

'So he's an unreliable witness but you still want us to question him and find out what he really saw? That doesn't make much sense to me, Nick.'

I can feel the weight of McKenna's comments pressing down on me. Tasha's face is a composition of confusion, frustration and hurt.

'Why would you believe him over me? I'm the one whose daughter has gone missing. Look into his record, alright? Just look into him and then tell me you believe his word over mine.'

'We have,' McKenna says, adding another layer of atmosphere to the room. 'We've looked into his record and we've looked into yours. His is clean.' She leaves it hanging in the air for a few seconds before speaking again. 'Now do you want to tell me everything?'

17

The car feels like it's rolling into corners far more than it usually does, but I know the problem isn't mechanical – it's the result of the substances that are swimming around in the chemistry of my brain. I've only been legally old enough to drive for just over a year, but I feel an enormous sense of confidence as I take the bends on the country roads with relative ease.

I grip the steering wheel tightly, my knuckles slowly turning white. I can feel the blood pulsing at my temples; a strangely irregular rhythm. I keep repeating her comment over and over in my head. That was where things started to go wrong. It was derisive, almost mocking me. And I don't think she was joking. From there, everything she said began to turn the screw, slowly grinding away at me until I couldn't take it any more. There was no argument – just a growing knowledge and acceptance on my part as to what I was going to do tonight. Once the red mist had descended, that was it. There was no going back. Once I step over the line, I stay over the line.

A slight feeling of nausea starts to rise up from my stomach, but I manage to push it back. I know it's because of a number of things – adrenaline, alcohol, drugs and a huge amount of excitement. I know the excitement is perverse, but that doesn't stop it from feeling good. It's the sense of knowing that you're about to get justice.

Over the past couple of years I've been writing a lot of poetry and some short stories. In one, a man is kidnapped from his bed, taken out to the woods and tied to a tree, where he's left to reflect and atone for his sins. I had the idea in the early hours of the morning a couple of months back. I couldn't sleep, couldn't relax. So I went for a walk. I know the woods like the back of my hand, and they were strangely peaceful at that time of night. I didn't feel any of the menace or unearthly feelings that might have been expected. I felt comfortable, lucid.

I really get into the heads of characters when I'm writing. I become them. I feel their pain, their anger, their elation. I like it. It means for a few short hours I'm no longer me. When she made that comment earlier tonight, I was transported straight back into the mind of the kidnapper in my short story. He's silent as he waits for the right moment, calm as he carries out his business, does what he has to do. But inside, a fire is raging. He thinks of all the things this person has said and done to him over the years. And he knows he's about to get his justice.

I glance into the rear-view mirror, just for a second. Her head is lolling about, her chin bashing off her shoulder as her weight pulls against the seat belt. I chuckle at the realisation that I actually went to the length of sitting her up in the seat and putting a seat belt on her. At least she can't say I didn't look after her.

As I steer the car off the road and into the opening between the two copses, I switch the headlights back to just the sidelights, trying to make sure I don't attract any more attention than I need to. I slow the car – I need to, because of the lack of light – and drive in a little further until I find the perfect spot.

I kill the engine but leave the car's sidelights on. I'm going to need to see what I'm doing. The soft glow of the car's lights illuminates the tree like a shining beacon.

I get out of the driver's side and walk around to the back of the car, opening the door and releasing her seat belt. I struggle to get my arms under hers and haul her out of the car, but eventually I manage it. She's a dead weight. Her shoes make two loud knocking noises as her feet slip off the back seat and against the metal of the car as I drag her out, before there are two much softer sounds of them hitting the mud.

I smile inwardly as I become the character in my short story again. I feel everything he feels: the anger, the sense of unjustness, the growing pleasure at the imminent restoration of justice. It gives me the extra strength to do what I know I need to do. I drag her the few extra feet from the car to the tree and place her down on the ground before going back to the car to fetch the rope.

It takes me an eternity to prop her up against the tree and free my own hands to focus on the rope. Even though she's only small, she feels like she weighs five times what she usually does. Eventually, I manage to lean her backwards against the tree at an angle and lock her knees, which stops her falling down just long enough for me to tie her hands behind the tree and then tie her feet to it. At that point, I know she's going nowhere. I lean forward and plant a kiss on her forehead. I don't know why, but it seems right.

Before I realise it, I'm back in the car and I've restarted the engine. It purrs into life beautifully, greeting me like an old friend. The headlights flicker as the engine starts and I look over at Angela, her head resting on her chest. The first thought that comes into my mind is that she'll have a sore neck in the morning. Maybe I'll pop by with some painkillers. Maybe I won't.

18

NICK

'It was years ago,' I say, closing my eyes and wishing this whole situation would go away. 'It's not even relevant. I was a different person back then.'

'It's very relevant, Nick,' McKenna says. 'And I want to hear it from your point of view.'

Why? I want to say. *So you can tell me which aspects of that don't match what you've been told by other people?* I wonder whether this is a deliberate ploy from McKenna, asking me in front of Tasha, trying to find out if I'm the sort of guy who'd keep something like this from his wife. She's just found out that I am.

I've never kept it from Tasha, exactly, but it's just not something that's ever come up in conversation. It happened in a dark period in my life, and it's not something I've been keen to talk about at any point.

'What is she talking about, Nick?' Tasha asks. This is what I really don't need.

Tasha and I have never really been talkers. There's a lot of stuff I haven't told her, but it's for her own good. I know how she reacts to things. And I know that the police know what happened. Now I have no choice. I swallow hard and take a deep breath.

'I had a girlfriend. Angela. It was years ago. I'd totally forgotten about it,' I lie. 'It was a stupid, immature relationship that should have ended long before it did. We both drank too much and smoked too much shit and one night things got too heavy. I did something stupid and that's the end of it.'

'What did you do?' Tasha says, quietly.

I swallow and shake my head. I'm ashamed to even recall it. It's not something I've sat and thought about for a long time. I've changed so much since then, it seems pointless. Looking back, it's like seeing someone else's life. Someone who preferred drinking and smoking drugs and living the good life instead of being responsible. Someone out of control. 'I waited until she'd drunk so much she passed out, drove her out to the woods, and tied her to a tree and left her there.'

Tasha's mouth hangs open as she blinks at me.

'I know. It was fucking stupid. I got pulled over on the way back home. Obviously I blew over the limit so I was taken in. When they asked me where I'd been, I told them. Apparently that's the only reason I got a suspended sentence instead of time inside. I was banned and fined for the drink-driving.'

Tasha makes a small choking noise. 'Oh my god. That's why you didn't want to go to America, isn't it? You wouldn't have got in.'

I nod without looking at her. 'I was young and stupid. And I was bloody lucky, too. Another judge might have sent me down. But believe me,' I say, holding eye contact with Tasha for as long as I can, seeing the tears misting her eyes, 'I have never done anything like that before or since. That was the last time I got drunk.' I look at McKenna. 'Other than the occasional glass of wine every now and again, I barely drink.'

'That's why?' Tasha says, quietly and delicately.

'Yeah. That's why. Because I never wanted to become that person again. When I drink I get stupid. That was the line in the sand, Tash.

That was when I became the new Nick.' I look at McKenna. 'And that's why it's got absolutely nothing to do with what's happening here and now.'

'I'm afraid the law doesn't quite see it that way,' McKenna says. 'As things stand, what happened yesterday morning is your word against your neighbour's. And he doesn't have a history of violent crime.'

'I don't have *a* history,' I say, stressing the word. 'It was a one-off incident. Years ago. It *is* history.'

'You have a criminal record, Nick. For a violent crime. I'm not saying your word's any less valid than his, but you've got to look at it on paper. We don't know either of you personally so all we've got to go on is what we see.'

I take a deep breath and pace towards the window. 'Well, can you not just take my word for it, then? I'm telling you the truth here. You might not know me but Tasha does, and Tasha knows I wouldn't lie.'

I turn to look at Tasha, but deep down I already know what I'm going to see. She's looking at me, the tears still misting her eyes, and she says nothing.

It's McKenna who speaks. 'Nick, I'd like you to come with me.'

19

NICK

I feel like it's all over. As though whatever happens now, they're always going to suspect that I'm somehow involved in Ellie's disappearance. That makes me want her back even more desperately, knowing it'll clear any suspicions they have about me.

I think back to what the police said about mirroring my laptop and mobile phone. I wonder how that works, whether the emails to and from Jen Hood can be seen or whether the police just see what was on each device at the time they mirrored it. I know I need to be much, much more careful from now on. No more contacting Jen Hood from my mobile or laptop. I'll need to think of something else. I've got the email address the messages were sent from memorised – not that I'll ever be able to forget a single pixel of that first email for the rest of my life.

The problem is, I'm not the most tech-savvy bloke in the world. I can find my way around, but for all I know I could have landed myself up shit creek and not known about it.

I can't blame the police. I was hoping they wouldn't find out about the Angela incident, but now they have I've got to deal with the consequences. I need them to believe that was the one and only time anything like that ever happened. They have to believe that. Otherwise, things are going to get a whole lot tougher and I'm even less likely to get Ellie back.

It's not that I think they're going to find out anything else about me. It's that the time they'd be wasting digging around in my past is going to detract from their efforts to find Ellie. I don't even want police officers going to the toilet or blowing their noses – I want them all out there, pounding the streets, knocking on doors, doing absolutely bloody everything they can to find my daughter.

The police station isn't far from where we live, but it seems to take an age to get there. Again, this is all wasted time as far as I'm concerned. I know that every minute counts when a child goes missing, and every minute lost makes me more and more desperate to have Ellie back with me.

The thought has crossed my mind that it might be someone from my past who's taken her. There aren't many people from my past who'd dislike me enough to do something like that, nor be unhinged enough to actually do it, but I do wonder whether Angela might be one. The problem is that she always seemed so meek and innocent. She never said boo to a goose. The drink and drugs were her way of letting her hair down and not having to live constantly under the watchful eye of her parents.

People change – I know that more than most – but I really can't imagine that Angela would've become some sort of deranged psychopath who goes around kidnapping children. Then again, did I ever really know her? We weren't together long enough. Which leads me to assume that she'd have no reason to track me down and kidnap Ellie. The last I heard, she'd moved to Australia. I can't see that she would have come back from there to deal with the pissing rain and heavy traffic here.

It was a stupid thing to do. Even to this day, I still don't know why I did it. I vaguely recall her saying or doing something and the 'red mist' descending. In those days, I wasn't the sort of person who was able to deal with anger very well. I used to react. Why I reacted in that particular way, I'll never know, but it's been hanging like an albatross around my neck ever since, and things are only going to get worse now that it's come out.

Oddly, what Tasha thinks of the whole thing just doesn't concern me. I know she'll be livid, which is her way of covering up the fact that she's actually devastated but unable to show her real emotions. She's always been the same, trying to put across this image of a strong, powerful, career-oriented woman. It's all an act, though, and sooner or later she's going to have to break. There are some things that even the strongest people can't handle.

Coupled with that, I know that this will probably end up breaking us. I've seen the statistics on how many married couples whose children are kidnapped or killed actually end up divorcing not long after. It's a lot for any marriage to handle, and ours has never exactly been the strongest. Plus I know Tasha will never forgive me for what happened with Angela. I can already hear her words in my head. *It's the fact that you didn't tell me. How could you keep something that big from me? I had a right to know.*

The problem with Tasha is she thinks she's got a right to all sorts of things. She thinks she's got a right to put all of her time and effort into her bloody job and to expect everyone else to fawn around her.

We had a huge argument about six months ago, not long after Ellie started at school. I made the mistake of calling Tasha selfish, accusing her of putting Ellie's development at risk by never being there. Sometimes I think Ellie would be better off with me as a single parent rather than nominally having two but never knowing when the other one will be coming home. Uncertainty isn't a good thing for a five-year-old girl. It's not great for anyone.

And it's the uncertainty of what's happened to Ellie that is killing me now. I'm a planner. I like to know what's going on. And right now I have no idea what's going to happen next. I don't even know if the police are taking me in to talk about Angela or about Ellie. Part of me doesn't care – Angela was years ago and I can't help them with Ellie. That's the problem: they're meant to be the experts at sorting out things like this, and I'm losing confidence in them with every passing minute.

I think back to the emails from Jen Hood. And a growing part of me wonders whether there might be another way out of this.

20

NICK

They tell me I'm not under arrest, but that it's a formal interview. I don't know what the difference is, and right now it doesn't really matter. The journey to the police station took place in stony silence. Out of the corner of my eye I occasionally caught McKenna glancing at me in the rear-view mirror, perhaps looking for some giveaway or telltale sign.

The interview room is much as I'd expected, but perhaps a little more comfortable. The chairs are padded and there's a carpet, which is a start. There are cameras in all four corners of the room, leaving nothing uncovered. I don't feel nervous, but I really don't want to have to go into any greater detail about what happened with Angela. It was stupid. I know that. But it was a long time ago and it has nothing to do with what's happened to Ellie.

'You've got to see things from our point of view, Nick,' McKenna says. I want to tell her I do. 'Your five-year-old daughter goes missing. You tell us you put her in the car and went back inside. Your sole witness tells us you didn't. You react by ransacking the man's house. We dig a little deeper and find out you've got previous for abduction.' She leaves that hanging in the air for a few seconds before speaking again. 'Do you have any idea how many missing children turn out to have come to harm at the hands of a family member?'

I shake my head. I don't know the exact number, but I know it's a lot.

'Most of them,' she says, pausing again before she leans forward towards me and clasps her hands. Brennan is sitting beside her, watching me with great interest.

'Nick, if you want to tell us something, you can. We always find out what happened eventually. Modern policing isn't about *if* we catch the perpetrator; it's about *when*. The longer things drag on, the more difficult it's going to be for you and the rest of the family to deal with what's happened.'

I raise my head and look her in the eye. 'Nothing has happened. Everything I've told you is true. I don't know where my daughter is, I don't know why Derek's lying and I don't know any more about anything than you do.'

Okay, so that last bit wasn't quite true.

'What are you hiding, Nick?' McKenna asks, throwing me off balance. I must have given away some slight involuntary twitch, as Brennan cocks his head to the side and raises an eyebrow.

'I'm not hiding anything,' I say, sounding a little like the lady who doth protest too much. 'Like you said, you'll find out what happened eventually. You've already been through my phone, laptop and car. What more do you want?'

'We want the truth, Nick.'

I laugh. 'I can't help you with that. I'm afraid that's your job. What have you found in the car, exactly? Hmm?' McKenna says nothing. 'What about on my phone? My laptop? Anything at all? No. Nothing. So what the hell am I here for?'

'We've been through this, Nick. We have every reason to treat you as a person of interest.'

'No. No, you haven't,' I say, feeling increasingly agitated. 'My daughter is out there somewhere. She's five years old. I don't know if she's alive or dead, and we're here, wasting time investigating the one person who cares most about Ellie in this world, rather than actually finding her and catching the bastard who took her! Or would that give you lot too much paperwork to actually get off your fucking arses and find her? I mean, why the hell would I report her missing if I had something to do with it? Have you asked yourselves that?'

'Calm down, Nick. We've allocated all the resources we possibly can to—'

'No, you haven't!' I interrupt, now shouting. 'You two are meant to be leading this investigation and you're doing the square root of fuck all. Why has it all dropped off? You were so good at first, and now everything's gone quiet. Why's that? Where are you focusing your efforts? On bullshit like this, that's where. If you think I'm hiding something, arrest me. Arrest me and hand me over to some pen-pusher to take a statement from me, then lock me up for twenty-four hours. That's what you're allowed, isn't it? At least in the meantime you can get on with actually trying to find Ellie.' McKenna and Brennan say nothing. They just look at me. 'Well, go on. Are you going to arrest me or what?'

There are a few moments of silence before McKenna speaks. 'You're free to go, Nick.'

21
NICK

Brennan dropped me back home and decided it would be a good idea to leave me and Tash alone for a while. A nice touch. Light the blue touchpaper and retire; hope that everything comes out without them having to do a full day's work. I don't know if it's just the stress of the situation, but I'm getting more and more cynical with every passing hour.

'Why didn't you tell me?' Tasha says eventually.

'I didn't hide it from you,' I reply.

'Don't dodge the question,' she says. I'm surprised by how calm and level-headed she seems. In a way, that makes it all so much more disturbing. I can only think of two other occasions in the whole time I've known Tasha that she's gone beyond the fury and despair of a situation and settled in this weird trance-like state.

'I didn't *not* tell you. I mean, when would be the right time? Over dinner one night? During the adverts in *Coronation Street*? At the altar just before we got married, perhaps?'

'I had a right to know, Nick. I gave my life to you,' she says through gritted teeth.

'And you wouldn't have done if you'd known about that? About one stupid, idiotic incident. Not even one whole day but one evening, one small, stupid incident that I've regretted ever since? You never knew that Nick. You know the Nick who's stood in front of you now. The family man who's only a family man *because* of that incident. Because it changed me. It made me who I am today. Personally, I'm grateful for that, and you should be too.'

Bad move, Nick.

'Grateful? You want me to be grateful?' Tasha shrieks, a full two octaves higher than she's been speaking so far. 'Nick, I have given my life to you. And now I discover that you're, what, a violent criminal?'

I bury my face in my hands and make a noise that sounds like an Olympic weightlifter going for the world record. 'You know exactly who I am, Tasha. I haven't hidden anything. Not deliberately, anyway. Don't you understand that? When I look back on my life before that incident, it's like an out-of-body experience. It's like I'm looking down on someone else's life. Like I'm watching a film. I didn't hide what happened; I just completely blotted it out. I wanted to forget it. I needed to forget it.'

She looks up at me and sneers. 'Are you honestly trying to tell me that in all the time you've been with me you've never thought about that night? Not once?'

I sigh. 'Of course I have. It's passed through my mind. Of course it has. But it's not like I think of it every day and go out of my way to make sure you don't find out about it, is it?'

'What about America?' she says, a lightbulb going on in her head. 'That would have been the perfect opportunity to tell me. You could've said "We can't go to America because I've got a criminal record. I did something stupid a long time ago and now I'm going to tell you all about it." But you didn't, did you? No. You made up some stupid excuse about work, deadlines and money. Try telling me you didn't hide it from me then, Nick.'

'I didn't,' I say. 'I mean, yeah, of course that had a bearing on things, but work was a factor in—'

'*Stop, Nick!*' she shouts. 'Face it. You lied to me. You lied because you didn't want me to know the truth and because you couldn't handle the truth yourself. Just like you can't handle the truth that you fucked up yesterday. Majorly.'

'I know I fucked up, Tasha. Christ.' How many ways does she want me to say this? Does she not think I feel like shit about what's happened to Ellie? That I don't blame myself? All I want is Ellie back here with us, safe and happy, and Tasha playing the blame game isn't helping things in the slightest. I know I fucked up.

'Do you? Do you, Nick? Because I don't think you do.' Her nose is now just inches from my chin and she's looking up at me, sneering, her eyes bloodshot as the spittle flies from her mouth. 'I don't think you get it at all.' One corner of her mouth lifts as she snorts and leaves the room.

Moments later, I hear the bedroom door slam and I close my eyes. I realise pretty quickly that sitting here on my own in the quiet isn't going to do me any good, so I look for distractions.

I head into the kitchen and pour myself a glass of orange juice. I look up at the Rosie Ragdoll. I used to forget it was even up there, sitting on top of the clock, but ever since Ellie disappeared I can't walk into the kitchen without seeing it, seemingly ten times larger than usual, staring down at me.

The temptation to throw a slug of vodka into the glass is overwhelming, but I resist. Taking two large gulps of juice, I wipe my mouth and head into my study. My laptop's still on, so I lift the lid and log back in. Before long, I wish I'd gone for the vodka.

There's an email. Another one.

Half of me is screaming to open the email as quickly as possible, but the other half is holding back, worried about what I might find. Eventually, I take a deep breath and click the email.

There's no text; just a photo of Ellie. I know instantly what it is. I know every single photo we've ever taken of her, and this isn't one of them. This is a photo that her abductor – Jen Hood – has taken.

My vision starts to blur as the tears well up inside my eyes. The picture fades until it's barely recognisable. I blink and the tears roll down my cheeks, making the picture clear again. She's clutching a toy that I don't recognise – a traditional-style teddy bear. She's sitting in what looks like a loft or attic. What hits me the hardest is that she looks happy. She's smiling.

My head's pounding and I really don't know how much more of this I can take. My mind is a swirling smorgasbord of confusion, and every extra thought just adds to the effervescent pot. It's dim and cloudy and I can't see anything clearly. In my confused state I feel oddly angry at Ellie. If she hadn't gone missing, if she'd only come home, then we wouldn't be in this mess. We'd be happy again.

I guess the stress and anger I'm feeling isn't really directed at Ellie. I'm angry at myself, and I'm angry at Tasha. What I need right now is her support. We need to support each other. Already, I'm beginning to see why so many couples in situations like this end up divorcing. This growing culture of guilt and blame is pure poison.

If I could swap Tasha for Ellie, I'd do so in a heartbeat.

I think back to the first email I received from Jen Hood, and in that instant I know what I must do.

22

TASHA

He doesn't get it. He doesn't realise that he fucked up and caused all this. That's what upsets me the most. If I thought there was even the slightest chance that one day he might understand, that'd be okay. That'd be a glimmer of hope. Something to work towards. But with Nick there's nothing. I sometimes wonder whether he's autistic or something.

It was a very strange feeling taking the medication again for the first time. I was transported back to those dark days, yet I felt oddly soothed by it. It provided some sort of solace, a reminder of a time when things were horrendous but at least they were sure. I knew where we stood. Now there's nothing.

I pull the duvet over my head and enjoy the darkness. *Enjoy* sounds like an odd word to use, but the darkness is comforting. It's holding the outside world at bay, not visible and not audible. I'm cocooned within my own safe environment, sheltered from everything else. For a fleeting moment, I feel as if nothing can harm me. Nothing's changed – Ellie's still missing and my marriage is still falling apart – but just briefly I feel as though I'm protected from it. As if I can leave it all outside, sit in here and breathe calmly, and then return to it all when I'm ready.

The feeling doesn't last very long, though, as my intense frustration and the thoughts whirling around my head start to intrude once again. There's a huge amount of anger, and I'm not sure where it's really being directed. Is it at Nick? At the police? At myself? At Ellie's kidnapper? At Ellie herself? I really don't know. All I know is it hurts like hell and there's not a thing I can do about it. It's the helplessness that hurts the most. Being able to do absolutely nothing to help your own child is the worst feeling in the world. I feel like I've failed as a mother.

Nick's deception hasn't helped. And that's what it was. A deception. It sounds horrible saying it, and almost antithetical to everything I thought I knew about Nick, but there's no other word to use. I can understand him not telling me as soon as we met, I'll give him that, but he had plenty of opportunities after that. When I was trying to organise a trip to America would have been the perfect time. But no, he had to come up with some bullshit excuse about work.

But it's not just the fact that he didn't tell me. Of course it isn't. I know deep down that my anger at Nick keeping this from me is just a cover for the fact that it frightens the hell out of me to think that my husband could have been capable of something like that. Even so far back in his past. Can a leopard ever really change its spots? He says he was in a bad place back then and that things are different now, but I'm not so sure.

He's not been in a great place for a long time – not since *Black Tide* – and that impacts negatively on all of us. I know writing isn't a steady job for most. I knew that when we got married and I've accepted that, but sometimes I feel as though that respect could go the other way, too. My job isn't just important; it's vital when his pay packet varies so wildly from month to month.

The truth be told, the financial aspect of our lives scares me. I used to be quite good at keeping an eye on our bank statements, but I've not looked for months. Possibly longer. The longer I leave it, though, the harder it gets and the more convinced I am there'll be something horrible lurking there. Out of sight, out of mind. I presume things must be alright – I've not seen any red envelopes come through the door recently. Then again, I'm never around when the post comes. For all I know, Nick could be hiding huge amounts of debt from me.

The thought sounds ridiculous. I'd never thought Nick could hide a large secret like that from me. I never thought I might suddenly discover we were tens of thousands of pounds in debt. Because Nick never keeps big secrets, does he? But now I know that to be a lie, too.

23

NICK

There's an internet café about half a mile from where we live, so I decide to walk round there. I figure I should be able to get there and do what I need to do before they close for the evening. Even though the police let me take my mobile phone and laptop back, there's no way I'm taking my phone out with me. For all I know, they could be using it to track my movements, and that's the last thing I need. I need to tread as carefully as I possibly can, not arousing suspicion.

I feel naked walking around without my phone, but there's not much I can do about that. I'll be out of the house for less than an hour, if that, and I'll just have to use the excuse that I forgot it and left it at home if I'm asked. The police don't need to know that no matter how disorganised I am generally, I almost never forget my phone.

The town centre is pretty quiet, which suits me. It allows me to stay inside my little bubble, trying to work out what I'm going to say in this email. I know what I want to say, and I know what will happen if I end up saying it. But I need to be tactful, need to take seriously what this person writing as Jen Hood is actually saying. More than that, though, I need to start gently probing. I need to find out who is doing this and why.

It's the *why* part that confuses me the most. To kidnap someone's child in the first place you need to either really hate the person with a passion or be completely mentally deranged. From Jen Hood's emails so far, it's impossible to tell which camp she falls into. I can only assume it must be the latter, because I've never made mortal enemies with anyone. Not that I know of, anyway. As for Tasha, I can't be so sure.

I've tried racking my brains as to who could want to do this to me. The police asked if there was anyone I'd fallen out with work-wise. There isn't. I'm a writer. There's nothing to fall out over. They asked if it was possible that a 'rival' writer could be involved, and I just laughed. There's no such thing as a rival in this industry. If a reader sees two books that they like, they'll buy them both. They'll buy as many as they want to buy. And, let's face it, since *Black Tide* very few people have bought mine. If any writer was going to go on a jealous psychotic rampage against another, it'd be me doing it.

Black Tide was pretty huge. It came off the back of the urban horror boom a few years back. The tail end of the boom, anyway. It was actually my least favourite of four ideas that I pitched to my agent at the time. It was about a teenage girl in America who goes to stay at her aunt's beach house and discovers mutilated body parts being washed up on the shore. Pretty derivative and unoriginal, but I had a killer twist. It topped the bestseller charts in the UK and the US and made my agent and my publisher a lot of money. Me, less so. It got us a deposit on our house and I treated myself to a new car, but the success all faded pretty quickly.

There was a second book a year later, which was one I'd wanted to put out for a while. My agent and publisher were less keen, but I talked them round. Even putting *From the author of Black Tide* on the cover and adverts didn't work, and the book bombed. It didn't even sell out its advance. The reviews pages slated it. And that was the end of my relationship with that publisher. Since then, I've flitted between a couple of smaller presses who've done sod all to promote me and who've paid even less than I was getting before.

As far as a writing career goes, that's all pretty shitty. But I still don't think I'd be first in line to kidnap another writer's daughter, no matter how mentally unstable I was. No, there's got to be something deeper than that. Something far more disturbing.

When I get to the internet café, I pay for my time and log on to the computer. I open Internet Explorer, cursing as it takes an age to load (about 40p's worth of time, by my count), and then I set about creating a new email account. I need an anonymous, throwaway address that I can use to communicate with Jen Hood. One that I'll only log in to from internet cafés or other places where I can stay anonymous.

I set up an email address under the name of Simon Spencer and log in. I click to compose a new email message and sit staring at the screen for a few moments before I start typing, the words flowing.

> *Why are you so hell-bent on making me kill my wife? If you want her dead, why not kill her yourself? Besides which, why do you want her dead in the first place? What has she ever done to you? I don't know who you are, and I don't want to know. Ellie is a five-year-old girl. She needs to be with her parents. Why are you doing this to us?*

Even though I'd planned out every word in my head while I was walking down here, all of that is now gone, replaced by a stream of consciousness. My fingers can barely keep up with the speed of my brain as they clatter across the keyboard.

> *I can get you money. Whatever you want. But it's not fair of you to ask me to do this. I can't. Why would you want me to do it anyway unless you're trying to punish me? Are you trying to punish me? Why? What have I done to you? Who are you?*

I've only typed a couple of paragraphs, but I'm absolutely exhausted, mentally as well as physically. I know it's not just from typing the email – it's from having to process all these thoughts and to try and get my head around what's happening. It feels like an electric charge buzzing through my skull, a brew of confusion and screaming voices. I feel as though I'm going to wake up at any moment and find out this whole disaster was all a dream, but deep down I know that isn't going to happen.

Without even thinking twice, I click the 'Send' button.

I sit back on the hard plastic chair and stare at the screen. My eyes lose focus as I just sit, my brain draining itself of all thoughts and feelings. My eyes feel heavy and tired. My limbs even more so. I just want to stay here and let them come for me. I could do something stupid, get myself arrested. Get put in jail. Get away from all of this. Whoever's hiding behind the Jen Hood name would know then that it wasn't my fault. That I couldn't kill Tasha if I wanted to. That they wouldn't be able to get hold of me or email me. That they'd have to release Ellie and find another mug to do their dirty business for them.

Right now I don't even know if that makes sense. In my confused state, it seems like a sound plan. But I know I'm in no frame of mind to be making any sort of plan. I know this is exactly what Jen Hood is counting on – throwing me into utter confusion and disarray and hoping I'll do something stupid. That's what this is all about. This person doesn't want Tasha dead. They want me to try doing something stupid and totally fuck it up, the same as I always do. Because I fuck everything up. That's who I am. That's what I do. That's Nick Connor.

I can feel my hands gripping the armrests tighter and tighter. I don't look down or even take my eyes off the computer screen, but I know my knuckles will be turning white, the plastic biting into my palms as I squeeze and squeeze, my teeth grinding and the veins beginning to show at my temples.

Then, at the apex of my fury and anger, there's a soft *ping* and a line of black text appears across one section of the screen. I'm looking at it but my eyes are still blurred, unfocused. I blink a couple of times, the letters starting to become clearer. I begin to be able to decipher words.

It's a reply from Jen Hood.

My instinct should be to open it as quickly as possible and see what it says, but my body and mind are still exhausted. With all the effort I can muster, I lift my right arm and drop my hand down on the mouse. I move the cursor across the screen and hover it over the subject line, clicking down on the mouse button. The email loads on my screen.

> *I don't want money. I want Tasha dead. And I want you to do it. It MUST be you. There is no other option.*

I look at it for a few moments, my eyes still glazed. What guarantee do I have that this person will return Ellie if I do what they say? They're clearly unhinged enough to kidnap a five-year-old girl and demand that her father murder her mother. What's to say that they're not crazy enough to kill Ellie, too? Is anyone crazy enough to murder an innocent five-year-old girl? All I know is that if I don't do it, Ellie certainly isn't safe. Not in the hands of this person.

I click the 'Reply' button. Much more slowly than before, but still as quickly as I can, I type out a response, knowing Jen Hood is sat in front of their inbox.

> *What about someone else doing it. I'll arrange it. If I try it myself I'll fuck it up and they'll find both of us.*

My breath catches slightly in my throat as I realise what I'm typing, but it's from an anonymous email address and I need to know what my options are. I click the 'Send' button.

I wait another minute or so, looking at the countdown clock in the corner of my screen that tells me how much time I've got left. It's now less than three minutes. Seconds later, a response lands in my inbox with another *ping*.

> *Do what you have to do. I don't give a shit about your child. You don't deserve her. If Tasha doesn't die, Ellie does. Believe that.*

At the bottom of the email, I can see a horizontal band of colour. It takes me a few moments to realise it's the top of a photo. I scroll down, the image revealing itself before me, slowly but surely. The background is a dusty brick wall, cobwebs softening the red brick colour. And there, at the bottom of the picture, looking down at something on the floor, is Ellie.

24
NICK

I've always wondered what would be the perfect murder. I guess many people have. The number of things that need to be taken into consideration is just extraordinary. But I reckon if anyone could do it, I could. I've spent years killing fictional people. Why not a real one? The fact of the matter is something that I've not wanted to admit, but which has been nagging away at me ever since I started receiving messages from Jen Hood. Most people would put their children above their partner or spouse. That goes without saying. But Tasha and I haven't been happy in a long time. She's selfish and career-driven, and she doesn't spend any time with either me or Ellie any more. How can she call herself a mother? Would Ellie even realise Tasha was gone?

But this can't be about emotion. If I'm going to get out of this, one way or another, it needs to be through clear, logical thinking. That's how so many people get caught: they let their emotions get the better of them and they do something stupid. That's how mistakes are made. And if I'm going to even consider Jen Hood's request, I know that I need to think logically and work out exactly what the possibilities and options are.

First of all, there's the method. Poisoning is generally out of the question in most instances, and anything quick and violent will be spotted as a murder straight away. Of course, that's not necessarily a problem if you have a convincing alibi and can remove yourself from suspicion. The husband is always at the top of the list of suspects, though, so that's something I'll need to think about very carefully.

In my confusion I'm finding it difficult to know what's right and what's wrong. That's a problem I've had a few times before, anyway, but it's never been more apparent than now. A large part of me is screaming to go to the police. But I know I can't. The threat from Jen Hood was pretty clear. If I go to the police, Ellie will die. I have to take that threat seriously: this person is deranged enough to kidnap someone's daughter in broad daylight. What's to say they have any sort of moral limits at all? Whoever it is, they're watching me. They've been looking at the house. They'll know if I speak to the police. They'll see the police coming from wherever they are, wherever they've held Ellie, and at the first sign of a flashing blue light or a suspicious-looking car, that'll be it. I can't risk that.

What's more, I have absolutely no faith in the police. I've been burned before, and I'm growing ever more disillusioned with the way McKenna and Brennan are handling this. I mean, I can see why they think they're doing the right thing, but that doesn't change the fact that I'm fuming that they've not even got the slightest lead on where Ellie is. Would me showing them Jen Hood's emails help find her? Possibly, yes. But it'd almost certainly mean the kidnapper would kill Ellie, and I can't imagine for one second they would have sent those emails in a manner that's in any way traceable. The police would be able to do nothing, and Ellie would be put in greater danger.

But there's one big thing that I absolutely cannot ignore. It's something that's been niggling at the back of my mind. Do I want Tasha gone? Would I be happier without her in my life? Would I be able to be me again? Do I even want to be me again? The me from before I met Tasha? Purely selfishly, yes I do. Tasha's not a nice person, but do I really want her dead? Between her and Ellie, there's no choice to be had.

I guess one thing on my side is the fact that my DNA will be all over the house and all over Tasha. We're married, after all. My fingerprints will be everywhere, as will my skin cells and strands of hair. The problem there would be if my traces were the only ones. That would just look unnatural.

Staging a break-in is too risky, especially with neighbours like Derek Francis. Something happening away from home opens up an unlimited amount of risk. What are the options? Cut the brake cables on the car? Not a great idea for so many reasons. The last thing I need is other people getting killed. And who'd cut the brake cables on a stranger's car?

It needs to either be a seemingly completely random killing – a mugging gone wrong, perhaps – or be made to look as though it could have been done by the same person who's taken Ellie. If I'm going to go through with this, the police must never know about the Jen Hood emails. I've deleted every email, which means they wouldn't find them if they were to go through my phone or laptop again, so now I just need to make sure they have no reason to look any deeper. I need to keep myself in the clear.

The mugging gone wrong is looking like a good idea right now. The only problem is, it can't be me who does it. I can't have the police sniffing around me any more than they have done. But if they do, and even if they later found the emails from Jen Hood, I need to make sure they can't prove a causal link. I'd need an alibi, and a rock-solid one at that. But who? We don't really have many friends – not ones who'd only see me and not Tasha, anyway – and it's not as if I go out to work.

A thought comes to me. Every evening at eight o'clock, Derek puts his rubbish out. He's a creature of habit. Every night he'll waddle down his path from the front door and pop a half-full black bin bag in the wheelie bin by the wall at the end of his front garden. If I could somehow make sure I was in full view of him at that point, there's no way he'd miss the chance to have a little nose at what I was doing. It would be wrong to say that Derek would be the perfect alibi, but he's all I have. There are no other options.

I think about this further. He failed to provide me with an alibi when I really needed one, but seems to be there watching when I don't want him to. All I need to do is make sure that he sees something he thinks I don't want him to see. Make him think he's got the power and the upper hand. I can't make it look like I want or need him to be my alibi – I have to make it look like him saying he saw me would incriminate me somehow. I can turn this all back on itself and use Derek to my advantage, but I have to think carefully about this. I need to be smart. If I could make Derek see something he thinks I didn't want him to see, then as long as I could prove I wasn't in the vicinity when Tasha was attacked, I'd be in the clear. And Derek would be my perfect alibi without even knowing or intending it. All I'd need then is some sort of hitman.

I almost laugh out loud at the thought. Listen to me, thinking of hiring a hitman to kill my wife, like some sort of Home Counties Al Capone. Would I look in the Yellow Pages under *H* for 'hitman' or *G* for 'gun for hire'?

This is going to need some thought. I know just how difficult it is to murder someone in the first place, never mind having to actually get away with it. The fact that I'll immediately be the prime suspect doesn't help, either.

But I can't help thinking back to that night with Angela. That moment of madness, which came completely out of nowhere. To have gone from being a perfectly normal, reasonable person to that absolute monster in no time at all. And as much as I try to justify it by saying it was a one-off, I know that in that moment I was capable of anything. I was capable of killing.

We all have that side to us. That point at which something snaps, whether reasonably or unreasonably. The cause doesn't matter. It's the result that matters. And I know that a person in that position is capable of doing some very dark, vile things. If I was capable of killing, Jen Hood will be capable of killing. Capable of killing Ellie. That's what worries me – the fact that I am acutely aware of what human beings are capable of when they think they've got justification for their actions. In this instance I don't know what Jen Hood's supposed justifications are, but they could prove to be the key. The fact is that Ellie's kidnapper will feel they had just cause for taking her. Whatever their rationalisation is, there'll be one. And if it's strong enough, there's no telling how far they might go, which is why I need to do all I can to find her.

The sun's starting to go down and my brain's getting tired. I reckon I've got a pretty decent chance of sleep tonight. That might sound odd, but somewhere deep inside my brain I realise I've come to a resolution. And there's no going back.

25

TASHA

The best thing about the medication is that it allows me to sleep, if only for a couple of hours. Last night, though, I don't think I even got that. I lay awake for most of the night, thinking about what Nick told me and the police about his former girlfriend. I know he doesn't drink or get involved in anything like that these days because he claims to have done his fair share when he was younger, but even I had no clue about his criminal conviction.

It scares me to think that Nick could have been capable of something like that. To think that it could just happen without warning and then never be spoken of again. What's to say it couldn't recur? What's to say it didn't happen again recently?

The worst thing is that he never told me. I thought we told each other everything. When I think back, I realise there are probably things I haven't told him, but nothing like that. And to make me sit there and listen to him telling me for the first time in front of the police, humiliating me and making me look stupid. What the hell was he thinking? If there's one thing I can't stand, it's lies, and I'm starting to wonder about what else he hasn't told me. If he can keep something like that from me for so long, what's to say he isn't hiding something else?

The problem with Nick is that he always keeps everything bottled up. He never comes to terms with his own issues and problems, and projects them onto other people instead. Add to that the fact that he's clearly capable of hiding huge secrets from his past, and I'm not sure that I even know my own husband any more.

For every waking minute since it happened, I've been racking my brain trying to think who could have taken Ellie. At the start, I hoped she'd just wandered off somewhere, perhaps tried to make her own way to school. By now, though, someone would have found her, taken her in and reported it to the police. Once it gets past a day or so, the police said we're looking at two possibilities: either someone's taken her and is holding her somewhere, or something horrific has happened and she's yet to be found. Every fibre of my being hopes it's the first option, but that means that someone has deliberately taken her, which leads everything back to *why*.

It's a question I know I can't answer. My brain won't even let me formulate any real possibilities right now. I'm struggling to put together any actual coherent thoughts. The lack of sleep isn't helping, and my head pounds with frustration and desperation. I feel like a fraud for even trying to sleep, knowing that I should be out there walking the streets, looking for my little girl. The police advised against it, telling us we needed to leave it to the experts, but that's easier said than done.

My brain almost defaults back to organisational and logical mode, and I decide I'm going to do what I usually do when I have to try and relax. The police have told us to try and retain some normality if we can, to keep us from going out of our minds, and when I need to relax and calm down I have a bath. Again, I feel like a fraud for even thinking about it, but there really is nothing else I can do at this time of the morning. The TV, radio and newspapers will be either full of reminders of people going about their normal everyday lives or carrying stories of

Ellie's disappearance. The police have passed on some information to the local press so people will keep an eye out, but I'm not sure what good it's going to do. If someone finds a five-year-old girl walking the streets on her own, they call the police regardless of whether or not the local fucking radio station tells them to.

I need to hold on to my last thread of rationality. I slide my legs out of the bed and make my way into the en-suite. I close the door quietly behind me and lean over the bath, turning on the taps and letting the steam rise as I inhale it. If I can shut all of this out for just a few minutes, pretend somehow that it isn't happening, I know I might just be able to keep a grip on reality. Because if I fall off now, I don't think I'll ever get back on.

26

NICK

The bright shaft of sunlight streaming through the curtains and hitting my eyelids like a laser beam is what finally wakes me up. I've slept right through. Amazing how the mind settles when you've made a decision.

I hear the sound of splashing water come from the bathroom at about the same time that I realise it's coming from above me. I go to sit up and feel the stiffness in my neck and shoulders. I'm on the sofa. I slowly get up and shuffle groggily up the stairs before heading into the bedroom, putting my ear against the door of the en-suite and knocking lightly with my knuckle.

'You in there, Tash?'

'Yes,' she calls, her voice echoing off the tiles.

There's a silence. 'Are you having a bath?' I call.

'Thought it might relax me.'

'Right. Good idea. Mind if I brush my teeth?' I ask, my mind only on the decision I came to last night.

'Door's unlocked,' she replies.

The handle squeaks slightly as I pull it down and open the door. The steam and smell of bubble bath hit me square in the face.

I look at her. Her eyes are closed and she looks as if she might be genuinely relaxing for the first time in a long time. I know her, though, and she's not a woman to forgive easily. The best way around her is to gradually reintroduce normality.

'You going to be in there long?' I say, grabbing my toothbrush and squeezing a large slug of toothpaste onto it.

'I need it. I can't just sit around thinking about what's happened to Ellie and worrying about you. All I'm going to do is make myself ill again.'

It's the first time in years Tasha has alluded to her breakdown. The last time we even spoke about it was when she'd gone up for the job in London and I'd worried that the increased stress would spark something off again. She'd assured me that it wouldn't, and said that if it did she'd jack the job in straight away. Up until now, she'd been right.

I mean, she'd been under more stress than usual just recently – before Ellie disappeared – what with the merger going on at work, but she'd seemed absolutely fine to me. Still, you never quite know what goes on inside a human mind. Since her breakdown, I'm not sure I really know Tasha at all. To see someone collapse so spectacularly, seemingly out of nowhere, can really make you question your own judgement.

A thought enters my mind, but I quash it very quickly.

It all started around the time we were told the IVF had failed and that our chances of ever having children were very slim. Tasha had been trying to put on a brave face, but I could see that she was collapsing inside. She tried to cover it over by burying herself in her work – her usual way of shutting out the outside world – but even Tasha, the woman with a heart of stone, couldn't pretend that nothing was wrong.

It was a Thursday. I remember it well. I was upstairs in the study, writing. I get my best writing done first thing in the morning while my mind is fresh. It's about the only thing I can get done in the morning, albeit at a time that I consider to be morning. Tasha's definition is what I would call still the middle of the night. I heard the familiar sound of Tasha opening the front door, then the sound of the door closing again.

The same as every morning. A few minutes later, I went downstairs to grab another cup of coffee and found Tasha curled up in a ball on the kitchen floor. She'd opened the door to go to work, but had been unable to face the world. Everything had finally caught up with her, and she'd realised that she couldn't bottle it all up.

I've never seen her like that before or since. She's usually such a strong person that she crosses the line into riding roughshod over everyone else's feelings. It hit me hard to see her like that. One of her friends recommended that she see a doctor, which she did. Personally, I would have suggested she see someone sooner than that. I could see the signs much earlier but presumed she would just deal with it in her own way, like she always does. If I'd suggested it to her she would have bitten my head off. I think it was good for her that she finally realised she needed help.

She took medication for a while. Some sort of antidepressants or tranquillisers. It was strange seeing her so subdued, so completely apathetic. It was almost as if nothing I could say would rile her. It was actually quite spooky. It enabled her to cope with life, but she wasn't the same person. She'd started to reduce her dosage already by the time she found out she was pregnant with Ellie, but that compelled her to stop taking them altogether.

The realisation of actually being pregnant was a strange one. We couldn't quite believe it at first, but when we finally got our heads around it we were keen to do whatever we could to make sure the baby would be happy and healthy. We took no risks. Apart from Tasha continuing to go to work – something I told her I wasn't happy about – everything seemed to be going well. It looked like it was going to hold us together. And then she began to change.

'You heard anything this morning?' I ask, before I rinse cold water around my mouth.

'Not yet. They said they'd call if they had anything. All we can do is sit tight. I'm going to go stir-crazy if I just sit staring at the walls. I need to try and get my head straight. Could you do me a favour? Plug the bedside radio into the extension lead and bring it in here, will you? I could do with some musical accompaniment. I need to drown out this noise in my brain.'

'Will you hear the phone if it goes, though?'

She looks at me as if I've just landed from another planet. 'I can't answer the phone from the bath anyway, can I? I was hoping you might be able to manage that.' Her look is playful, but I doubt her intentions are.

Having untangled the wires from behind the bedside table, I bring the radio in and rest it on the edge of the sink unit. I freeze momentarily as I see the opportunity in front of me.

One of the many things Tasha has been nagging me about is getting the house rewired. Over a year ago we had an electrician in to fit a new double socket in the kitchen. He happened to mention that the house uses an old wiring system and isn't properly earthed, nor is the fuse box fitted with an RCD, which would trip the circuit and stop you getting a serious electric shock if there was an electrical accident. Not a major problem in itself, but something that needs doing – granted. As far as Tasha was concerned, though, the house could catch fire and burn down at any minute, and she spent the next couple of months going on about how we should get the whole house rewired as if it was some small, insignificant job I could do in a Saturday morning. I don't know much about electrics, but I know it's not a small job.

I try to use my minimal knowledge of electrics to work out how much voltage runs through a digital radio. A hairdryer in the bath? Sure. A portable heater, even. Would a digital radio do the job? A large part of me doubts it, but I'm still faced with the opportunity to find out once and for all.

Does this fit my plan of the perfect murder? Perhaps. I wouldn't necessarily be suspected, would I? After all, it's difficult to run someone a bath, force them into it and lob an electrical appliance in without them putting up some sort of a fight. It's not foolproof, but it'd take a hell of a lot of doing to try and convict me of anything. Could they somehow find out when the radio was unplugged from the wall and then plugged into the extension lead? The clock sets itself from a digital receiver, so there's bound to be some sort of trace somewhere along the line. Could they cross-reference that with the temperature of the bathwater or the amount of wrinkles on her skin and work out that she couldn't possibly have brought the radio in for herself? It seems a little far-fetched.

The most likely outcome is that very little would happen other than the radio dying and Tasha at best getting a zap no stronger than she would from licking a battery. Then how do I explain lobbing a radio into the bath with her? It would need to look like I'd done it accidentally. Perhaps nudge it with my elbow or hip as I walk past. Or lean over to give her a kiss and . . . Whoops! No. Too risky. I wouldn't want to be in contact with her or the water if I've got even the slightest suspicion that there's going to be 240 volts knocking about. Physics was never my strongest subject at school, and right now I wish that I'd listened more carefully.

There's only so many times I can pad at my face with the flannel before she's going to wonder why I'm still standing here, staring at the radio and at the water. If I'm going to do this, I need to do it now.

I take a deep breath and place my flannel back on the sink unit, just inches from the radio. I fold the flannel carefully in half, then into quarters and pat it down with the palm of my hand. I'm stalling for time here, I know it.

I turn and look at Tasha's naked body lying in the bath, her eyes closed, her hair pooling around her neck and breasts, swaying in the water. She opens her eyes and smiles at me.

'I'm sorry. I do love you, you know, Nick?' she says.

I swallow. Hard. 'I love you too.'

I force a smile and leave the room.

27

NICK

I know what media appeals are all about in missing persons cases. Especially when they concern missing children. McKenna told me it would help to publicise Ellie's disappearance and ensure that people kept an eye out in case they saw her or had any information as to where she was. That's all bullshit, though. Most people couldn't tell one five-year-old from another.

There's only one real reason why they do national media appeals when children go missing: it's because they've got a suspect. And not only do they have a suspect, but they have a suspect sitting behind the desk doing the media appeal.

That's why there'll always be the random uncle, grandparent or family friend doing the media appeal with the parents. They want to see how their suspect reacts in front of a camera. Whether the crocodile tears come out. The police psychologists will be watching with their notepads at the ready, analysing every last twitch of an eyelid, every casual scratch of the nose.

Except this time there's no uncle, grandparent or family friend behind the desk. There's just me and Tash. And I know who I've got my money on as their prime suspect.

McKenna knows this, too. She knows that I know. She's not stupid. When she told us about the media appeal she watched me with the anticipation of a boxer watching his opponent as the opening bell rings, ready for the first sign of a twitch. Of course, I told her I thought it'd be a great idea. Anything that'd help find Ellie. And I meant it, too, even though I know the chances of the appeal leading directly to her being found are extraordinarily slim.

Before I received the note, I'd have had no concerns. Now, though, I know exactly what's going to be on my mind throughout the appeal. It'll show on my face, too. It can't not. If that's interpreted by the psychologists as some sign of guilt, it could be curtains. All of the police's resources will go into investigating me, trying to pin something on me in connection with Ellie's disappearance. That doesn't bother me one bit from a selfish point of view, as I had nothing to do with it. But it does mean that they won't be looking in the right places, and that makes it even less likely that Ellie will be found.

It's too late now to tell them about the Jen Hood emails. If I'd gone to them at the start, there would have been a tiny, wafer-thin possibility that they might have been able to track down who sent them. But since the kidnapper told me he'd kill Ellie if I told the police, I'm not going to take that risk. And now, with the time that's passed, even if I did manage to find a way to tell them without putting Ellie at risk, they'd want to know why I didn't tell them earlier. They'd look at my responses and decide I was going to go through with it. I'd become complicit. Could they do me for withholding evidence? Probably. I don't know. But what I do know is that – as bizarre as it sounds – Ellie is actually safest where she is right now, as long as the kidnapper believes I'm going to do what he wants me to do. That gives me a little breathing space to try to get to the bottom of who's doing this, or for the police to find him through their own means.

Just being innocent isn't enough. Knowing you're a suspect is what kills you. Any of us who've ever been in the same room when someone has discovered their phone or wallet has gone missing will know exactly what that feels like. Even though you know nothing about it, everyone knows there's a chance it could be you. It's a weird kind of awkwardness; a guilt with no reason to exist. But surely the psychologists would know that, wouldn't they? The rational part of my brain that tells me so is being gradually worn away.

It's all been arranged in a bit of a hurry, from what I can tell. I mentioned something of the sort to McKenna, but she told me it was important to do it as quickly as we could to maximise the chances of Ellie being found safe. 'The first few days are the most important,' she told me, as if I didn't already know. She also tried to assure me that they'd done this a number of times before, and for me not to worry. The paranoid half of my brain tells me they do it that way to put their suspect under pressure. No time to prepare. Just sit him down and put him in front of a microphone and a camera and the nation's prying eyes.

I don't even know if it's going out live or just being recorded for the evening news programmes. They've told me very little, considering I'm her father. That makes me immediately even more suspicious. I know I've got to put that out of my mind, though. Right now, I'm the father of a little girl who's been snatched away from her parents. The focus is on finding Ellie alive and well.

McKenna opens the appeal by introducing herself and DC Brennan. The metallic insignia of the county police force sits proud on the temporary fold-out wall behind her as she leans forward purposefully on the desk, her hands clasped together.

What sickens me the most is that they've given me a pre-prepared statement. And not one pre-prepared by me, either. It's one they've 'had to word carefully to maximise our chances of success', McKenna told me. It sounds more like a marketing plan than an appeal for a missing child's safety, but I roll with it. It's all part of their game.

Tasha looks at me and I take her hand in mine. I look out over the desk and make eye contact with a journalist. He holds it, just for a moment, and then looks down at his notepad as he scratches his ear. He knows, too. He must've seen this a hundred times before. He knows the drill.

I'm not even listening to what McKenna says, but I notice she's stopped talking and is looking at me. Tasha nudges me slightly. I blink a few times, unfold the sheet of paper on the desk in front of me and start to read from it.

'Since Ellie disappeared, our lives have been torn apart,' I say, not sure how much emotion I should be putting into this. 'Our little girl has been a constant in our lives for the past five years and all we want is to have her back home, safe and well. If you know where she is, we wish you no harm. We just want our little girl back.' *Wish you no harm? I want to rip your fucking head off.* 'Ellie, if you see or hear this, please let somebody know you're safe. You're not in any trouble, sweetheart.'

My voice cracks as I speak those last words. It sets Tasha off, which sets the flashbulbs of the press's cameras off. That's the money shot for their front page, they'll be thinking. A great shot of two grieving parents. That's what they want, isn't it? Build the drama, sell the papers. It doesn't matter how much of it is real.

And, right now, I don't know how much of it is real.

I comfort Tash, my brain only really processing the noise of the cameras firing and flashing. Somewhere amongst the maelstrom, McKenna's words rattle, distant and faded.

'. . . if anyone has any further information, to call our incident room on . . .'

I close my eyes and try to push it all away.

28

TASHA

In many ways, the media appeal feels like a huge load off my mind. A weight off my shoulders. But then in other ways it feels like an enormous burden, as if we're now under the watchful eye of the British public. I can't help but think of the way in which the newspapers and the public have turned on victims in the past. I keep thinking of the Madeleine McCann incident and the way her parents have been vilified by certain people ever since. She was snatched from her hotel room in Portugal while on holiday, and her parents had to suffer the ineptitude of the Portuguese authorities and the venom and bile of the British gutter press. I pray to God that doesn't happen to us.

I know there'll be people who already suspect we have something to do with it. There always are. The police warned us of that prior to the press conference. They told us not to go on social networking sites, not to watch the news and to keep our minds focused on finding Ellie. They didn't need to tell me – I know there are some sick bastards out there and I certainly have no intention of allowing them to make me feel any worse than I already do. Not that anybody could.

Opening it all up to a wider audience does have its advantages, of course. The idea is that more people will be on the lookout for Ellie and it might even scare the kidnapper into giving himself up. One thought which did occur to me, though, and which I'm struggling to shake, is that it might scare him into doing something stupid. If the media attention were ever to achieve the sorts of levels that the Madeleine McCann case did, there's not a kidnapper on earth who'd think he could outsmart everyone else in the population. As much as I hope – desperately hope – that the media appeal will help find Ellie and bring her home again, I can't help but worry that it might force the kidnapper's hand the wrong way. All we can do is hope and trust in the police that they're the experts and will help bring Ellie home.

Nick's not so sure. He's always been more sceptical. It's probably the writer in him. He was furious after being taken in by the police, but I know a lot of that was him projecting again. He's angry with himself. Deep down he knows he was in the wrong, both for leaving Ellie in the car and for keeping the Angela thing from me. I'm flickering between wanting to comfort my husband and wanting to watch him stew in his own misery, and that's not healthy for any marriage.

I couldn't say anything at the media appeal. What could I possibly have said? I can't even understand my own feelings, let alone put them into words. I veer from anger to anguish, panic to desperation. But the overriding feeling is a sense of confusion. None of it makes any sense. Everything was fine, everything was normal. We had no warning. Things like this don't happen to people like us. How can a perfectly normal family be having a perfectly normal day and then see their world turned upside down within a few seconds? And why? That's the biggest question. But I can't help thinking about Angela. Nick says there's no way she's responsible, but I'm not sure if I can believe him. How can I, after everything he's kept hidden from me? How do I know he's not trying, in his usual pathetic way, to protect me from things he thinks are going to hurt me? If he really wanted to do that, he could have started by looking after our daughter properly.

The problem is that there isn't anyone else. We don't really have enemies in our lives. There's certainly no-one unhinged enough to take our daughter. Which just leaves the possibility of the passing opportunist. It sounds so cold and clinical to say it like that, but it's better than having to face up to the *P*-word. I know Nick has suspected Derek, but I can't see that, either. The police have searched his house and found nothing.

Either way, Nick needs to control himself and stop flying off the handle. What kind of lunatic goes and ransacks an elderly man's house on a hunch? That's something else that's got me worrying about Nick. Up until the last day or two, I would have said he doesn't have a violent bone in his body. Yet within the space of a few minutes I find out that he's turned over our neighbour's house and that he kidnapped a girl years back.

Kidnapped. It's that word again. The one that won't disappear. The one which, up until recently, seemed so prosaic and ordinary despite its negative connotations but which now carries the weight of the world on its shoulders. I just can't seem to shake it. Nor can I shake the surprise that Nick's name keeps cropping up alongside it. Whichever way I look at it, he's admitted to having abducted a girl in the past. Yes, he was drunk and under the influence of drugs, and yes, he says it was a one-off. And I believe him. Why shouldn't I? After all, what possible reason could he have for wanting to kidnap our own daughter? There is no reason that I can think of. Media attention? A PR stunt? A cry for help? None of those make any sense. Nick has undoubtedly seemed unbalanced recently, but that's only since Ellie's disappearance. And anyway, who wouldn't be slightly unhinged after their daughter's been kidnapped? It's a perfectly normal reaction. Isn't it?

29

NICK

I feel strangely cautious about conducting any sort of research on my own computer now. The police have returned the car already but didn't bother to do me the courtesy of letting me know they'd found nothing. Even though it's back, I can't shake the thought of the car being tracked or followed. So I slip on my shoes and leave the house, deciding to walk into town.

My first port of call is the library. I go inside and speak to the young girl at the desk about using their public computers. She tells me I'll need to sign up for a library membership. Yeah, I know. A writer who doesn't have a library membership.

Apparently it only takes five minutes to sign up. All I'll need to do, she says, is type in my identification number and password and I can then use the computer. I don't like the sound of this. The last thing I want is my research activities being logged against my name by a public body.

I want to avoid using the same internet café as I did the other day. I don't want my face to be recognised. I need to keep covering my tracks. The problem is, internet cafés aren't quite as popular as they were.

I know there's an internet café in the next town. At least there was six months ago when I last drove past. It's a good five miles away, but I decide I could do with the walk, anyway.

When I get to the internet café, I push the door open and walk inside. There's no-one in here other than the man, who I presume to be the owner, sitting at a desk at the back of the shop. I'm not particularly surprised – who uses internet cafés when everyone has a computer and smartphone these days?

I walk up to the man and ask if I can book some time on the computers. I hand over my money, and he points me in the direction of a terminal.

I wait an age for Internet Explorer to actually open – this is why I use a Mac – and I eventually get around to being ready to type in my search terms. Fortunately for me, my screen faces the wall, so I don't have to worry about the prying eyes of the shop owner or anyone passing by on the street.

I sit for a few moments, not actually entirely sure what it is I want to search for. My brain feels like it's full of fuzz, unable to formulate any clear thoughts. I try to think back to the mindfulness exercises I've done in the past and remember some of the techniques, but no matter how hard I try I just can't shift the fog.

I pull a notepad out of my bag and start to doodle. A few minutes later I've still typed nothing into the computer but have created a brainstorm, with the word *MURDER* in the middle and all manner of ways of killing someone stemming from it. So far I've covered strangulation, electrocution, blunt force trauma, stabbing and 'accident', complete with inverted commas.

Although I've spent years writing about people dying in all sorts of horrible and gruesome ways, when it comes down to it I can't shake the thought that I'm not going to be able to do it myself. The ideas I seem to be favouring are what one might call the indirect methods: 'accident' seeming particularly enticing.

I turn a page on my notebook and continue scribbling. It's mostly just a stream of semi-connected words and thoughts.

Car problem? Staged disappearance. Note or letter – would need to be foolproof or could tell forgery. Long-term plan?

The words seem to make sense as I write them, but they very quickly become nonsensical. One thing I do know from my writing career is that the perfect murder requires one thing above all others: meticulous planning. No aspect can be left unthought of. The way my mind is right now, I'm in no state to commit the perfect murder. Not on my own, anyway.

30

NICK

The long walk home gives me plenty of thinking time. My new way out might seem like the easiest option but it's fraught with its own difficulties. If I'm going to get someone else to do my dirty work, the obvious first question is *who.* The *how*, I can leave up to them.

A thought has been rattling around at the back of my mind for a little while now, but I've been reluctant to address it. An old school friend of mine did time once. I say an old school friend because we've barely seen each other since then, but we used to be thick as thieves. Best mates. Neither of us was a model pupil, but Mark Crawford was something else. He was never violent or aggressive, but he had a real rebellious streak.

Mark always used to have a way round anything. He wouldn't do anything on the straight and narrow and had a good eye for a competitive advantage. If we were playing cricket in PE, he'd have a key tucked into the waistband of his shorts, perfect for carving ruts and divots in the ball to make it spin more unpredictably. And he was the only kid I knew who didn't pay any attention in class and still managed to sail through exams. There had to be something dodgy about that, too. There was always something dodgy where Mark Crawford was involved. By the time he was twenty-two, he was banged up for organising an elaborate VAT money-laundering scheme involving a closed circle of limited companies he'd set up purely for that purpose.

We'd not really met face-to-face much since school, but the joys of Facebook, which admittedly I only use very rarely, meant we were able to keep in touch. I'd never really told Tasha much about him. If she knew his history, she'd only judge him before she'd even met him, so I'd never bothered going into detail. All this was irrelevant right now, though. The only thing at the forefront of my mind was that Mark Crawford knew people. Bad people. People who might be able to help me out of this mess and get Ellie back.

I'd love nothing more than to have faith in the police right now. But the problem is that I can also see things from their point of view. A young girl disappears, and no-one sees her go. Add to that the fact that the prime witness – a 'reliable' witness with no chequered past – says the dad never put her in the car to begin with. Who's suspect number one going to be? Yours truly. I grind my teeth as I think about Derek.

Anyway, where do you start looking when you don't even know which way she went at the end of the driveway? The logical next step is to try to work out who might have taken her, and then to work out from that where they might be.

I have to make them see that Derek is lying. That they're wasting so much precious time looking at me when they could be finding her.

The sum of it all is that the best the police can do is wander around cursorily looking in bushes and putting up posters. There's been talk of putting on more pressure through the media, but they're worried this might scare whoever has Ellie into panicking and harming her. When they put this point to me, I strongly agreed. After all, I know someone has her and that that person might well panic, as they suggested. I couldn't tell them that, though.

I'm not going to lie – I've often wondered what life would be like without Tasha. I've always said that if I hadn't settled down and got married I'd probably be out travelling the Far East or Australia right now. I certainly wouldn't be mortgaged up to the eyeballs in the same bloody town I grew up in with no hope of ever getting out. In so many ways, things would be a lot easier if Tasha wasn't around.

We couldn't go off travelling now. Not now we're married with a kid and a mortgage, not to mention the rest of the baggage that goes with it. Tasha's not exactly likely to want to give up her precious career, either. But me and Ellie, just the two of us? Yes, that'd work. Especially if we had nothing left to stay for.

Another thought crosses my mind. Tasha's insured. That was something she'd insisted on when we first got married and bought the house. We even made sure to include provision for any children we had, with extra money being provided for their care if one of us were to die. Do insurance companies pay out in cases of murder? After all, I've got to assume that might be the verdict if I can't make it look like an accident. No. I push this thought from my head. I *have* to make it look like an accident. Either that or a murder I couldn't possibly have committed. I could sell the house, add the insurance money in, and Ellie and I would be able to live fairly easily roaming the world. I could even hire a tutor for Ellie to come with us.

These thoughts seem fantastical because they're so far removed from what we're used to, but when you sit down and work it out on paper you realise just what simple things you'd have to do to change your life completely. If you want to, that is. Up until Ellie went missing, I'd probably have done the same as most other people and just carried on as I was. The easy option, I guess. But now there's absolutely no question. I'm in no position to let things carry on as they are. Now, things *have* to change. I need Ellie back.

Mark once told me about a local guy who'd befriended him in prison who claimed he could do him 'a favour' if ever he needed it.

My fingers grip tightly around my phone in my jeans pocket as I walk, knowing that as soon as I take it out and dial Mark's number, I'll have made a serious move. Right now, though, to me, it doesn't seem serious. What seems serious is the fact that my young daughter is missing and in the arms of some crazed psychopath. To get her back, all I need to do is make a phone call and have my sham of a marriage ended, leaving me free to live my life as I want to, with my daughter back with me. Free to be without cares or worries.

Would I really be free, though? What happens when Tasha dies? The police would suspect me, surely, but I could prove that I didn't do it. They'd definitely suspect that I was involved somehow, and they'd probably know that I organised it. But they'd need to prove it without reasonable doubt. They'd need evidence. If I'm careful, I can make sure they've got no evidence.

I think about the best way to call Mark. The safest option would be to go to a phone box or use someone else's phone, but I decide against it. If the police really wanted to, they'd be able to find out I called him. And how then would I explain calling him from a phone box? On the face of it, there's nothing suspicious in me calling him. We went to school together, we're linked on Facebook and I've got nothing to justify. The police would have to prove something, whereas I could simply say I was phoning a friend. I don't have many, so why not Mark? Going to a phone box would just look more suspicious. Besides, it's not going to be Mark who does it, anyway.

Before I realise it, I'm scrolling through my contacts to *M* and tapping Mark's name. I bring the phone to my ear and wait for the familiar tone of the call to start buzzing. Mark picks up after four rings.

'Nick! How's it going, mate?'

'Yeah, good,' I lie. 'Well, not great actually. Listen, are you in town? I can't really talk on the phone.'

'Christ, mate. I don't think you've phoned me for about six years, and now you phone to say you can't talk on the phone?' He laughs.

'I know. I'll explain it all in person. It's just easier,' I lie. Fact is, there's a decent chance my phone's being tapped into, especially if the police see me as a suspect in Ellie's disappearance. It'll be bad enough trying to explain why I'm phoning a convicted criminal for the first time in six years just after my daughter goes missing, but I've got an – admittedly weak – excuse for that. 'I'm having a shit of a time at the moment and my head's all over the place, so I'm trying to write as much as I can to keep myself sane. I need to pick your brains for some research. I'm writing something set in a prison, and, y'know . . .'

'Hah, yeah, I know. No worries. I'm just heading back from the station at the mo. Can meet you in Jubilee Park in five if you like.'

I smile. This is where we'd always go after school to feed the ducks in the pond.

'Sure, see you then,' I reply.

31

NICK

Mark is already sitting on the bench overlooking the pond when I round the corner into Jubilee Park. He's slouched against the slatted wooden back, eyes closed, face pointing up towards the warm sun.

'Sorry, sir, we don't allow vagrants to sleep here,' I say as I walk up behind him and clap him on the shoulder. He chuckles, immediately recognising my voice.

'How's it going, mate?' he says, extending his hand as I sit down beside him.

'Been better,' I reply.

'Yeah, saw all the stuff on Facebook. Grim. Can't imagine what you must be going through.'

'Neither can I,' I say.

'Rozzers got any idea where she might be?' Mark asks.

'Not a bloody clue. Unsurprisingly.'

'Some things never change. Your head must be all over the place.'

I try to stop myself laughing. 'Yeah, you could say that.'

'So what's this research you're doing?' he asks, sensing that I want him to change the subject. I don't.

'To be honest, mate, I'm not doing any research. I kind of had to say that on the phone as I reckon the police might be tracing my calls.'

'Shit, why? Ellie?'

'Yeah. They've been asking me weird questions. I suppose the family are automatically the first suspects, but it doesn't exactly make me feel much better.'

'What kind of weird questions?' Mark asks.

'I don't think they really believe what I've told them. Trouble is, the old bloke who lives across the road seems to have some sort of issue with me. He clearly saw me put Ellie in the car but he told the police he saw nothing. So it's basically my word against his. And he's some sort of pillar of the community it seems, while I . . . Well . . .'

'The Angela thing?' Mark asks.

'Yeah. Exactly.'

'Don't worry about it, mate. They always try that route. If you've so much as had a copper knock on your door in your entire life they'll try and hold it against you. Just rise above it.'

'Easy for you to say,' I reply, leaning forward and resting my elbows on my knees. 'Listen, mate, I know we haven't really spoken for years but I can still trust you, right?' I notice a look on Mark's face. 'Christ. Fuck, no. Nothing like that. Jesus. I can promise you now I had nothing to do with Ellie's disappearance. But I received an email. A ransom note.'

I tell Mark what the email said. I can remember every word, every punctuation mark.

'Fuck,' he replies.

'Yeah, exactly.'

'You reckon it's genuine?' he asks.

'Put it this way. The person who sent it was outside my house. They made some comment about the policeman stood on my driveway.'

'Wow,' Mark says, looking out at the pond. A mallard duck bobs under the water for a couple of seconds, as if shielding his ears from our private conversation.

'Yeah. Listen, I don't need the lecture or the matey advice. I've been thinking about it a lot. If I have to choose between Tasha and Ellie, there's no choice to make. Only . . . Well, you mentioned something a long time ago about a bloke you know who could do favours,' I say, immediately regretting the daft gangster-movie language.

Mark, quite rightly, laughs. 'Wait, so you don't speak to me for six years, you pop up days after your daughter goes missing and you're suspect number one, and now you want me to put you in touch with a hitman so you can pop off your missus? You been smoking something, mate?'

I swallow hard. 'I know it sounds mad. But I know deep down that whoever has Ellie won't get her back to me unless I do this. They'll kill Ellie unless I do what I need to do. The police haven't got a hope in hell of finding her. The only evidence is the email and if I give them that, whoever's got Ellie will kill her. I can't risk that. How can I? I mean, fucking hell, the thought of Tasha dying . . . But that's nothing compared to thinking about life without Ellie. I couldn't bear that.'

'So bumping off your wife is a better option?'

'Yeah, it is,' I say flatly.

'Jesus.' Mark looks out across the pond, his eyebrows raised slightly as he leans forward, rubbing his hands as if rinsing them under an imaginary tap. 'I dunno. I mean, this isn't the sort of shit I want to get mixed up in, you know?'

'He's a friend of yours, isn't he?' I ask.

'Depends what you mean by "friend". I know him, yeah. But I wouldn't invite him over for chicken chasseur and a game of Trivial Pursuit.' Mark shakes his head. 'Look, I'm a white-collar man, yeah? I don't get involved in any of this stuff. I'm not a violent man.'

'Neither am I,' I say, turning my head to face him. He just raises one eyebrow. 'That was a long time ago, Mark. You know that.'

'Yeah, I know, sorry. Just a bit shocked, y'know?'

'I thought you were unshakeable?' I say, with a wry grin on my face. Mark always prided himself on being a man of the world – an honourable criminal, as some might have said.

'Well, it's not every day you have a conversation like this, is it? Listen, I'm not going to get involved, alright? I ain't organising anything. If you want to get in touch with a bloke and do a business deal, that's your problem. But it's nothing to do with me. Got that?'

I swallow and nod quickly. 'Yeah. Thanks, Mark.'

'Guy's name is Warren MacKenzie. Drinks in the Talbot Arms. He's got a couple of Serbian lads who work for him, have done for years. Reliable, like. No-one knows who they are except him, and that's the way it's got to be.'

This all seems so surreal. The fact that it's just like a scene out of a gangster film almost makes me chuckle. Part of me wonders whether Mark's fucking with me and trying to sound like Don Corleone because he's on the wind-up. But I've known Mark for a long time, and I can see in his eyes that he isn't. For the first time, I think I see fear.

32

TASHA

Nick's been out for a couple of hours. I don't know where – he said he wanted to clear his head. The media appeal is due to be shown on tonight's news, so we're not likely to have much space after that. I didn't know until afterwards that there'd be that delay. I presumed it would be shown on all the news channels straight away. Every second counts, and getting that message out there to everyone as quickly as possible is vital as far as I'm concerned.

The police told us they had to be careful and make sure they released the information in the right way and in the right order. I wasn't sure what they meant by that, but I can only assume that they've got some leads they're following and want to use the media appeal to control that somehow. I feel almost violated that they're not passing this information back on to us, particularly as it's our daughter that's missing. I have no idea how much they know or what they think they know, but you'd think that telling us would be a priority. Unless we're under suspicion.

I'm not going to say that the thought hasn't crossed my mind. Of course it has. If you're thinking logically, you'd probably expect some tricky questions. But for me, all I can feel is a sense of sheer desperation. These people are meant to be helping us bring Ellie home. They've told us time and time again to leave it to them. They're the experts, they say. Yet if there's even one percent of their time spent suspecting us or investigating what we're doing, that's time that's being taken away from finding the person who really took Ellie.

It's amazing what changes when something like this happens. Everything you thought you knew is altered. Ordinarily, I've never been one for talking. Like Nick, I tend to keep my feelings to myself. Neither of us has really ever opened up to the other. I don't think that's ever caused a problem, but ever since Ellie went missing I've needed him there for me. If not him, someone else. As if I've been bottling it up all that time and now I just need someone to offload onto. Someone who's shown some sort of care and attention recently. Someone female. Someone who isn't a bloody police officer.

I decide to call Emma. She's been in touch a couple of times recently and she knows I'm struggling because she helped me get the doctor's appointment. She always seems to be available and at the end of the phone, too. Someone I know I can rely on. And in that moment I feel disappointed in myself that I've not been a good friend to her. We've been friends, of course, but of the Christmas-card-and-occasional-chat variety. The sort of friends that most adults have, I guess. We've never been particularly close, but right now she's all I have.

She exudes calmness from the moment she picks up the phone. That's one of the things I like most about Emma – that she always remains relaxed and reassuring. She asks immediately how Nick and I both are and if there's been any news regarding Ellie. I tell her there hasn't been. Before long, the ever-astute Emma realises something is wrong.

'Is there something on your mind?' she asks, knowing full well that there must be. She knows I'm not the sort of person who phones people up for a chat.

'Yeah, one or two things,' I say, almost sarcastically. As if my mind were going to be free and clear right now.

'You know you can talk to me, don't you?' Emma says. 'I know we're not as close as we used to be, but I'm always here if you need to talk.'

'I know,' I say. 'Thanks.' And she's right. We used to be pretty close at university. The four of us were. We all fitted nicely into the stereotypes: I was the ringleader, the strong, confident one who got most of the male attention; Emma was the quiet, unassuming, slightly hippyish one who'd been convinced to go to university by her parents but had no intention of using her degree other than to keep them happy; Cristina was the one who'd drink far too much and end up disappearing halfway through the night, either back home or back to someone else's home; and Leanne was the dedicated sporty one who didn't drink, looked after herself but was still capable of having a good time. I lived at home with my parents as the university was only about three miles away. Emma was from Droitwich, Cristina had come from Wales, and Leanne from Devon. It was a group that just seemed to gel. They all stayed and settled in the area after uni, which led us all to believe that we'd be friends forever. I think that complacency was probably our downfall.

We all started to drift apart towards the end of our time at university. I'd met Nick not long before that. We met at the student union, even though he wasn't at the university. He had a few friends at the uni because he was local, too, and we got chatting as friends first, before getting closer. Even then, thinking back, he didn't open up. I'd never asked him if he had a girlfriend, what his background was, nothing. I wasn't an asker and he wasn't a teller. At first, we didn't even tell people we were together. We were acquaintances, then friends, and then it just sort of happened. We never felt the need to tell anyone. There wasn't even a starting point as such. I just remember being increasingly attracted to this arty, never-give-a-fuck sort of guy who was completely happy and comfortable in himself. There's something very sexy about a man whose self-confidence is just that and never boils over into arrogance.

'If I'm honest, it's Nick,' I tell her, cradling the phone closer to me even though no-one else is around to hear. 'He's making things worse by making this all about him. And his behaviour, it's . . . worrying.'

'Worrying? How?'

'A couple of things,' I say, trying desperately to think of how to word it all. 'You know what he's like. I can't work him out.'

'Why? What's he doing?' Emma asks.

I swallow. 'I don't know if I'm meant to be telling you this, but they didn't tell me I couldn't. He had this bee in his bonnet about the old guy across the road. He's convinced there's something dodgy about him. Something about him changing his statement or claiming he didn't see Nick putting Ellie in the car. Anyway, he went over and asked him. Reckoned this man knew where Ellie was. He frightened the life out of him, Em. He ransacked the poor guy's house. The police had to lead him away.'

Emma exhales. 'Christ.'

'And then he gets back home and the police are there, of course, and they start asking him these questions. Turns out he got a suspended prison sentence years ago for kidnapping his girlfriend at the time and tying her to a tree while they were both drunk and high.'

'Bloody hell. And this was before he met you?' she asks.

'Yeah. It's why he doesn't drink very often, apparently. I know he used to smoke cannabis and things before we got together, but even that was far less than he was doing when this all happened. And I didn't know a thing about it. How can someone just hide that from you for that long? As if he just forgot.'

'I don't know,' Emma says. 'People do, though. Would it have changed your view on him if you'd known earlier?'

I sigh. 'It depends how much earlier. Right at the start, if he'd come out and said, "Hi, I'm Nick. I abducted my last girlfriend," I probably wouldn't have hung around too long.'

'It might not have been his last girlfriend,' Emma says. 'It might have been ages before.'

'Might have been,' I reply. 'I don't know. I didn't get the details. I never asked him about his ex-girlfriends. I mean, who does?' As I say this, I realise I actually know very little about Nick's past. I know the basics – where he grew up, who his parents were, where he went to school. But never any details. Never any anecdotes. Never any fond stories and memories.

'Forgive me for saying it,' she says, 'but it sounds to me like you've got doubts about Nick.'

'I don't know. I really don't. I guess it's just a shock. I found that out, and then it all blew up. I couldn't cope. And now he's started going out, saying he needs some space. I don't know where he is, what he's doing. I don't even know if I want to know.'

'Is there anything I can do?' Emma says after a few seconds of silence.

'I doubt it. I just needed someone to speak to. There's the policewoman, Jane, but I don't feel I can really open up to her. I always feel like she's watching me, keeping an eye on me and waiting for me to do or say something wrong.'

'That's the police for you. I guess they're just doing their job. I wouldn't worry too much about it. If you ever need to offload, you can call me, okay? I'm always at the end of the phone.'

'Thanks,' I reply, not knowing what else to say. I think if I say much else I might be at risk of breaking down completely.

33
NICK

The Talbot Arms is a pub I've never been in before. I've lived in this town all my life and the pub's always been here, but I don't think I know anyone who's ever drunk in it. Put simply, it's the roughest of rough estate pubs; a concrete monstrosity covered in St George's crosses and Sky Sports banners. There's always at least one window boarded up, and you can smell the cigarettes and stale piss from a passing car.

The car park is strewn with dog-ends and lager cans, but there's a distinct lack of cars. I'm only inches from the door when I suddenly wonder what the hell I'm doing. This is a massive step to take. The fact that the kidnapper wants me to do this rather than hiring someone themselves tells me they want to make me suffer, too, which means it's someone that Tasha and I have both upset. That makes it even more impossible to work out who it could be. How do I know I'm not being set up? It's definitely possible, but the chances are slim compared to the likelihood of me never seeing Ellie again unless I go through with it. Anyway, what harm can a little chat in a pub do?

I push open the door and walk inside. My feet immediately stick to the carpet and I feel eyes on me. This isn't the sort of place that gets much passing trade and I must stand out like a sore thumb. I've got hair, for a start.

I walk up to the bar as casually and confidently as I can and order a lager. The landlord looks at me a second more than would be comfortable and starts pouring. 'Just moved in,' I say. Christ knows why. I get my pint of lager and pay for it. The landlord sits on a barstool a few feet away from me, glancing over at a group of four bald men playing pool.

'I'm actually looking for someone,' I say. 'Warren MacKenzie, his name is. Does he drink here?'

'Who's asking?' the landlord says, not taking his eyes off the pool table.

'I am,' I reply.

He slowly rises and walks over to me, leaning across the bar between two hand-pulls. 'And who are you?'

'I'm a friend,' I say, for some reason extending my hand as if inviting him to shake it. To my surprise, he does. 'I just need to speak to him. A friend put me in touch with him.'

'A friend put you in touch?' he says. 'I thought you said you were a friend.'

'Well, a friend of a friend,' I say, stuttering.

A wry smile rises up on the landlord's face, and his shoulders rise and fall as he makes a noise that sounds like a deep-sea diver clearing his snorkel. 'Warren. Bloke over here wants to see you,' he calls to the guys at the pool table.

One of them stands and walks over to me, not once breaking eye contact as he makes his way across the pub.

'Yeah?' he says as he reaches me. He's a big guy, and he's wearing a short-sleeved chequered shirt that makes it difficult for me to work out if it's muscle or fat. There's a tattoo protruding under the sleeve on his right bicep, but I can't quite make out what it is.

'Hi,' I say, extending my hand like I did with the landlord. Warren's not quite so accommodating, though, and ignores it, still not breaking eye contact. 'A friend said you do a bit of work and might be able to help me out.'

'Yeah, you need an extension building, then?' he replies. I can hear a quiet murmur of chuckles from his friends at the pool table.

I squint at him, unsure as to whether he's messing with me or if this is meant to be some sort of code. What should I be saying?

'I need help with a favour,' I say. It's all I can think of.

'Sorry, mate. Don't do favours. Paid work only. Price of bricks has gone up recently, you see.' The ripple of laughter from his mates increases.

'Look, can we talk outside?' I say. 'A friend sent me. Said you were reliable. It's probably best if we talk in private.'

'Oh, is it?' he replies, edging a couple of inches closer to me. 'Well, I don't agree. If you want to say something, you can say it here. Who's your friend?'

'I can't say. He asked me not to.'

He responds by making the same snorkel-clearing noise the landlord did earlier. 'You're lucky I'm in a good mood. Out,' he says, pointing at the door.

I can see the menace in his eyes and I'm not going to argue. I fucked that right up.

I open the door and head out into the car park, the soles of my shoes dragging against the tarmac. I sit on a low wall and close my eyes, feeling the sun beat down on the back of my head.

A few moments later, I can hear a metallic scraping noise. I turn and see the landlord repositioning an empty beer keg against the outside wall of the pub. He turns and looks at me before walking over.

'Don't worry about Warren,' he says. 'He's just being careful. It's his way.'

I force a smile and carry on watching the passing traffic.

'Why did you say you'd just moved in?' he asks, perching on the wall beside me.

I shrug my shoulders. 'Dunno. Didn't want to seem odd just walking in randomly.'

'Warren's had a few run-ins with the police. As you can imagine, he's suspicious of people he doesn't know. I've seen your face in the paper, though. I know who you are. Wait there a sec.'

Before I can really process what he means, he's gone. Fuck. He knows who I am. That doesn't help one bit. I have absolutely no idea if I can trust this guy. All I know is that it seems perfectly normal to him to have professional gangsters drinking in his pub, so I have to hope for the best. I can't back out now. I have no other option.

Less than a minute later he's back, followed by Warren. I stand and walk towards them as we meet in the middle of the car park.

'Richard tells me you're alright,' Warren says.

'Yeah. Sorry we didn't get off to a good start. Not exactly something I'm used to, all this,' I reply.

Warren gives Richard a look, and the landlord heads back inside, leaving the two of us together. Warren looks at me and waits for me to speak.

'I need someone taking care of,' I say, trying my hardest not to sound like a stock character from a gangster film. 'My wife.'

There's a few moments' silence before he speaks. 'Richard told me who you were. I'm going to level with you. Honour and trust mean a lot to me, you understand? I have my business model but I've also got my ethics. I don't go in for any of this shit that women are faultless. They're worse than men, usually. What's gone on between you and your missus is your problem. Not for me to judge. But I draw the line at who I help for different reasons, alright? Now. Look me in the eye and tell me you don't know what's happened to your kid.'

He makes it sound so threatening and difficult, but it's the easiest thing I've had to do for a long time. I look him in the eye. 'I swear I have no idea. I just want my daughter back. It's the only way to get her back.'

He nods.

'What do you do?' I ask. 'I mean, how long does it take? Is it violent? I need to know.'

'I don't know what you're talking about,' he replies with a neutral look on his face, although I can see in his eyes that what he's really saying is *We don't talk about this.* I understand he's being cautious, but there's no way he can think I'm possibly an undercover police officer or anything. I'm asking too many direct questions, for a start. It'd be the worst case of entrapment ever.

'How much do you charge for your . . . services?' I ask.

'Fifteen grand,' he says, without blinking an eye.

I try not to look shocked. 'Right,' I say.

'Cash, up front.'

'What, all of it?' I ask.

'That's what up front means. Despite what Richard says, I don't know you from Adam.'

What choice do I have? But if Tasha's found dead and there's a paper trail that shows me having withdrawn a huge amount of money, how am I going to explain that one?

'That's a lot,' I say. 'What's my story going to be for where all that money's gone?'

'Story for who?' he asks.

'For the police.'

'Why would the police ask? You keep your nose clean, buddy. You give them no reason to suspect you.'

I swallow. 'My nose is already a bit dirty,' I say.

His eyes narrow. 'Well, you'd better fucking clean it, then, hadn't you? This is my business. This is what I do. I can't go working with people who I can't rely on.' He must spot something in my eyes, because he stops and looks at me for a moment. 'Look, my brother's got a betting shop over on the Dunhill Road. Only takes cash. You know how it is. It's a traumatic time, you're weak, upset. You take to gambling. Horses, greyhounds, the lot. It gives you an escape, a quick buzz. Before you know it you've lost fifteen grand. Easily done.'

I see exactly where he's going with this. 'How, though? The police will know I never went into the bookies. They'll have CCTV.'

'You'd be amazed how often that CCTV goes down,' he says with a wry smile. 'But he's a reliable witness. Been in business about twenty years. Gives terrible odds, but he has a few regulars who like to spend their money there, if you know what I mean.'

'What, you mean money laundering?' I ask.

He shrugs innocently. 'I don't even know what the word means, mate. Now, can you get hold of fifteen grand or what?'

'Yeah. No problem,' I say. I quickly try to do a few sums in my mind. We've got some money in a savings account, but not much. The overdraft would probably get me an extra five grand, and I could probably withdraw some cash on credit cards. 'When do you need it by?'

'Depends how urgent the job is,' he says.

'Pretty urgent,' I reply. 'Thing is, it's got to be totally away from me. An accident or something.'

Warren nods. 'What sort of woman is she, your wife?' he asks. 'Does she work? Go to any evening classes? Hobbies?'

'Uh, not much,' I say. 'She works but doesn't do much in the evenings. It's usually late by the time she gets home. Why?'

Warren raises an eyebrow at me.

'Oh,' I say. I try to rack my brains to think of something. 'How soon can it be done?'

Warren shifts his weight to his left leg. 'How soon can you have the money?'

'As soon as you want it,' I lie. 'She's off work at the moment . . .' I trail off, hoping Warren will pick up and take control of the situation. Every word I say feels like poison.

'Go to the Crazy Chicken takeaway on Northway. It's one of my businesses. Buy something and ask them to pass on a letter to me. Give them a sealed envelope with a picture of your missus in it. Tell them your name is George and that you'll call back in to see me on whichever day you want it done. Got that?'

'I think so,' I say, trying to take it all in.

'Make damn sure you have,' he says. 'Do all that as soon as you can. Leave the money in the purple bin in the alley down the back of Crazy Chicken. Put it in a bag or something, for Christ's sake. I'm not fishing through there with my bare hands. Then immediately ring this number,' he says, passing me a plain business card with just a number and the word *John* printed on it, 'from a payphone. When you get an answer, ask for John. They'll say you have the wrong number. You hang up.'

'Right,' I say. My mind seems like a muddled mess, but I know damn well that I'm highly unlikely to ever forget a single word of this conversation.

'Whatever you do, only ring that number once. Never ring it again and never use my name. Got that?'

'Got it,' I say, swallowing hard. It seems incredibly daunting, yet ridiculously easy.

34

NICK

When I get home I secretly hope Tasha isn't there. All I can think of is visions of what's going to happen. But that's always where human beings fall down, isn't it? We don't like our current situation and we see the very distinct possibility of a perfect outcome, but we're never willing to endure what happens in between. If I were to offer you either a fiver or a punch in the face and then a tenner, which would you take? If you'd take the fiver, you're the same as most people. If you'd take the tenner, you're like me.

As soon as I walk in the door I can hear her voice. She's on the phone, but I can't make out who she's speaking to. I force a smile and lift my hand in a pathetic wave as I pass the living room door and head into the kitchen. I lean on the work surface, my palms outstretched as I stare at the coffee machine and will it to make a cup for me. I know the Rosie Ragdoll is there on top of the clock, looking down at me. I don't even need to look at it to know.

I can't make out what Tasha's saying from here, but I can hear the odd 'Yeah' or 'Well, that's the thing' through the walls. I've got to be honest: I like my peace and quiet. But it's going to seem strange not hearing Tasha's voice again. It all sounds so final, but then I guess it is. Death does that.

I don't know what's going on in Tasha's mind. I've always found it difficult to work that out, but now it's even harder. I've not got any point of reference. I don't think she's given up and believes that Ellie is dead, but it's her weird keep-calm-and-carry-on normality that's worrying me. With Tasha, this is usually a coping mechanism. She was like it when my parents died, too. She suddenly becomes very British and moves into organisational mode as her emotions almost shut down. I'm not going to lie – that sort of stability is what's keeping me grounded at the moment. Of course, that won't last for long. Not once she's dead.

My heart flutters, a surge of adrenaline hitting me as I realise everything is now almost out of my hands. Once I've done as Warren told me and I've got him the money, that'll be it. No more input from me. Nothing to do. Just sit and wait. That's both comforting and incredibly worrying.

Do I need to email Jen Hood to say everything's in hand? I decide it's best not to. Just in case. It'd be pretty stupid to send an email saying I'm going to have my wife killed. What I've sent so far wouldn't necessarily incriminate me in anything. I don't think so, anyway. But why hasn't Jen Hood been in contact with me to see if I'm going to do it? Why isn't there some sort of deadline? Is this a deliberate tactic to force my hand? Go quiet and hope I cave in?

The money. Fifteen grand. How am I going to get hold of fifteen grand in the days before my wife dies and not arouse suspicion? Drawing it out of the bank seems a stupid idea in retrospect, but I'm not exactly going to call Warren and ask if he takes payment in instalments.

To keep it untraceable and to fit the gambling story, I'd need to get cash, and ideally from a number of different sources. Only problem with that is there'll be more leads and witnesses. I can't sell the car because that'd look suspicious. Anyway, only recently it was considered a crime scene. I can just see the advert now: *One careful owner. Forensically declared free of child's blood.* Getting hold of fifteen grand without it being traceable isn't exactly something that can be easily done, though. Besides which, Tasha would probably notice fifteen grand missing from our account.

If you can't hide the money entering the system, you need to mask it leaving. This whole gambling story seems a bit far-fetched to me. Perhaps I could just mask a bit of it, or even the majority. But the whole lot? To go from non-gambler to fifteen grand in debt with the local bookies in the space of a few days doesn't quite seem right to me. It's fairly reasonable that a guy whose daughter has just gone missing and become the object of national scrutiny would have a fair few costs to bear. That's why people set up trust funds. As long as it was legal, how I got hold of the money wouldn't really matter if I made it look as though it was going to a cause which would be helping get Ellie back home. Strictly speaking, of course, it is, but I'm not entirely sure the police will see it like that.

I start to get grandiose ideas about carrying off some sort of bank job or heist but very quickly quash them. Experienced gangs attempt this sort of thing and get caught, so what chance do I have? Besides, the sentences for armed robbery and murder aren't all that dissimilar.

Fifteen grand. Christ. There's some cash in the safe in our bedroom – about three grand – which was meant to be our 'emergency fund'. Tasha had panicked a bit when the banking crisis hit and Northern Rock fell. We had some money in a savings account with them and managed to get it out, but she's been convinced ever since that we should at least have some emergency savings kept in cash. We're the only two who know it's there, and if Tasha wasn't around then it'd only be me. To anyone else, that cash doesn't exist.

Three grand isn't quite fifteen grand, though. It's only a fifth of what I need to get Warren to carry out the hit. That's when it hits me. I need fifteen grand to get *Warren* to carry out the hit. This town is full of desperate drug addicts and people who'd cut off their right arm for five hundred quid, so there's got to be someone who'd kill a stranger for three grand.

But how the hell does someone go about getting that organised? You can't exactly walk up to someone in the street, ask them if they're a drug addict and offer them some cash to murder your wife. This is getting ridiculous. The risks would be far too high. At least someone like Warren knows what he's doing. Like anything, you get what you pay for. At the end of the day, though, if you can't afford the very best then you're just going to have to make do with something that gets the job done within budget.

A whole host of ideas rattles around my mind as to how I can get this moving. I need to get it moving, because I need Ellie back. The problem is, my face and name are getting better known now, at least locally, thanks to the media attention Ellie's disappearance has garnered. If a local lowlife is willing to kill a stranger for cash, he'd certainly be willing to cough up and sell his story about it. I can't risk that. That leaves me only one option: doing it myself. Still not an idea I'm willing to entertain.

I think back to the risks of the killer opening up and telling all. That would only be a risk if it could be proven that it was me who ordered the hit. Sure, I'd probably be prime suspect, but if I had the perfect alibi for the time and had never actually come into direct contact with the killer . . .

Anonymity was what was needed, as well as a good way of covering my tracks. I remember doing some research a few months back into the 'dark web'; a corner of the internet hidden from search engines and most browsers, accessible only anonymously, and then through a series of proxy servers. Sounds complicated, but it's not.

If you or I connect to the internet on our computers, the computer connects straight to the internet service provider, which connects us to the website we're browsing. Using the dark web, there are tens, if not hundreds, of connections in between, bouncing from China to Canada, France to the Philippines. At each stage, a layer of encryption is added to hide the true source of the connection. Long story short, by the time you've connected to a website, your traffic has bounced around the world numerous times in the space of a second or two and has been made completely anonymous. If I could find a killer on the dark web, I'd be in business.

Even with the anonymity of the dark web, I can't risk using my own computer or internet connection. I've had my laptop returned to me, but it's still not worth the risk. I think of my most IT-savvy friend and give him a call.

35

NICK

Alan's back bedroom looks more like the Starship *Enterprise* than a place anyone would ever sleep. A tattered old dining room chair is the only incongruity in this place of flashing lights and high technology. He has four flat-screen monitors, two side by side with another two on top, leaning forward slightly to provide a nice curved effect.

'That's bad that they've not given you your laptop back yet,' Alan says, rummaging in a cupboard.

'Yeah, tell me about it. I'm going stir-crazy not being able to write, too. It's the only thing keeping me distracted at the moment.'

'I can imagine, man,' Alan replies. His upbringing had been very middle class, but he still had a bizarre manner of using colloquialisms and street talk which jarred with his voice. 'We've all got to have our creative outlets, you know what I mean? Ah, here we are.' Alan emerges from the cupboard with a black laptop, the power cable wrapped around it.

'Used to be my baby, this one. Quad-core Sandy Bridge processor and Radeon HD graphics. What a beaut. Getting on a bit now, but still good. Don't worry about rushing it back to me. I don't use it any more.'

'Great,' I say. 'Actually, do you reckon I could get some work done here for a bit? It's like a madhouse back at mine,' I lie. 'Phone going every five minutes and journalists knocking on the door. Just be nice to get back in the zone, you know?'

'Yeah, sure, no probs,' he says, slapping me on the back. 'Sit yourself downstairs at the dining room table if you like. Probably get some peace and quiet down there.'

'Actually, you might be able to help me,' I say, cradling the laptop under my armpit. 'I'm trying to write a cyber thriller. I've got a character who's meant to be one of these shady online arms and drugs traders on the dark web. I don't want to do too much poking around for obvious reasons, but I'd like to at least get the technical side of things right. Reckon you could run me through the basics?'

'Course. It's actually pretty simple,' he says, grabbing the laptop from me and flipping open the lid before switching it on. 'This has already got Tor on it, if I remember rightly. It stands for "The Onion Router". It's basically a browser you can use to access the dark web. They called it that because it creates layers of different connections around your browsing, to mask who you actually are and where you're connecting from.'

'And people use this for trading illegal stuff, right?' I ask.

'They sure do. It's all kept pretty untraceable, especially when they use bitcoin as their currency. It's a digital currency so there aren't any registered bank accounts or anything. Keeps it all anonymous and more or less untraceable.'

'That's mad,' I say, smiling and pretending that I don't already know this and am truly amazed.

'Yeah, totally. There are these places like the Silk Road, which is basically like an illegal version of eBay, where people just sell drugs and guns and people's credit card details and stuff.'

'Wasn't that shut down? I thought I saw something on the news.'

Alan laughs. 'Nothing's ever shut down on the dark web. It's a cat-and-mouse game, man. They shut it down, someone opens it again in a different place. No problem.'

'Crazy,' I say. 'What other stuff do people do with it? I mean, if they're trading stolen credit cards and guns and stuff, surely the sky's the limit for these sorts of people?'

'Yeah, totally. There's some really fucked-up shit. If you thought the internet was bad, the dark web is something else. If you think of the most fucked-up thing you can think of on the internet, that's basically pre-watershed compared to this shit.'

'How's it policed?' I ask casually.

'It isn't really. Well, I mean there's obviously coppers on there, knocking about trying to get information on who some of these people are, but the ones who are really careful can't be identified. That's the beauty of the dark web – you can only ever really identify yourself. If you want to stay completely below the radar, it's a piece of piss.'

The laptop has now booted, and Alan's opened the Tor browser and is busily scrolling through a list of websites. 'Here, try this one,' he says, clicking a link. 'It's basically an underground dark web version of Craigslist. If you thought the original was bad, this is just mental.'

I'm vaguely familiar with Craigslist, which is basically a catalogue of online classified adverts. Everything from second-hand cars to coin collections, right through to escorts and prostitutes. I had an inkling there'd be far fewer coin collections on this version, though.

'This is great, thanks,' I say. 'Should give me a few ideas and help keep it all realistic.'

'Yeah, good thing. I'm totally sick of the way all these books and films do the computer stuff, y'know? "Oh, let me just zoom in on that grainy image and read the inscription on the guy's ring." "Let me just tap the keyboard a few times and hack into NASA." It's all bullshit, man.'

I chuckle. 'Yeah, tell me about it. Mind if I go and have a browse? I'll keep away from the weird shit,' I say.

Alan laughs and sits back at his computer. 'You'll have a fucking job.'

36

TASHA

I'm going stir-crazy. Returning to work just isn't an option right now. The police have advised us not to read newspapers or watch TV. Sitting around and waiting is the closest thing to hell I can imagine. I'm spending most of the day on the phone, speaking to friends and family and keeping in touch with work colleagues. Even though they've all told me they're there if I need them and to call any time, I'm starting to sense that they're getting a bit bored of hearing the same stuff over and over again. But my brain can't handle anything else right now.

I've got to face that other people's lives are still going on. They're still coming back from work to their kids, still sitting down in front of the TV, still carrying on with their normal everyday lives. That seems perverse, and at the same time it makes me feel so angry and alone. How can people just go about their business, not caring? I know people mean well by trying to be nice, but how can they really understand what I'm going through? The fact is they can't.

My growing realisation that friends are starting to become less patient and supportive is something that really scares me. After them, what next? The media frenzy will surely die down after a little while. It always does. And then what? Will people stop looking for Ellie? Will the searches start to scale down? Will the police close the file and move on to the next missing child? And what about me and Nick? What happens to us? How do we deal with the fact that our little girl isn't coming home? Because, let's face it, the more time that passes, the less likely it is to happen. People will stop looking. People will stop caring. And I don't think I could handle that eventuality.

I've found myself punctuating the day with cups of tea. It helps a little to keep some routine, some reminders of how everyday life used to be. Not much, but slightly. And then I feel a deep sense of guilt and shame at even attempting to retain some sense of normality. But what is the right way to deal with this? There isn't one.

The doorbell goes. I instinctively peer through the curtains and look outside, but I can't see anything. I get up and walk over to the front door, using the spy hole to see who's there. It's Jane McKenna. I unlock the door and open it, letting her in without exposing myself to the outside air.

'Warm in here,' she says, before anything else. 'How are you, Tasha?'

'How do you think?' I reply, trying to sound pleasant but failing. She ignores it.

'I was just wondering if we could have a quick chat. There's no news as such, but I wanted to get a few things straight. Can I come through?' She gestures towards the living room.

I nod and she walks through, with me following closely behind. We sit down on separate sofas and she crosses one leg over the other, putting a notepad down on her lap as she taps a pen against it.

'How have things been between you and Nick?' she asks. 'In the last couple of days, I mean.'

I widen my eyes and sigh. 'It's hard. Obviously. What do you expect?'

'Is he in?'

'Uh, no, I think he went out. He came back briefly, but went out again.'

'Where is he?'

'I don't know,' I say, after a pause. I realise how odd this sounds. As if a wife wouldn't know where her husband was while she's waiting at home for news on their abducted daughter.

'Didn't he tell you?' Jane asks, in much the same tone as a concerned friend might use.

'Well, no,' I reply. 'Truth is, we've not exactly been talking much.'

She smiles benevolently. 'Have you spoken to the family liaison officer? We can put you in touch with people who can help there.'

'We don't need help, thank you very much. We need you to find our daughter.' I surprise myself with the tone that comes out. 'I'm sorry.'

'We're doing all we can,' she says. 'I know it might not look like much from this angle, but we've got a whole team of people working behind the scenes to find Ellie. These people know what they're doing.'

I nod.

'What about his friends?' she asks.

'What about them?'

'Is there anyone he sees regularly? Anyone he might have gone to see today? We just need to build up a bigger picture. You'd be surprised how it can help sometimes.'

I think for a moment. 'No, no-one. Not really. There isn't anyone he sees regularly or anything like that. He tends to keep himself to himself most of the time.'

'Tasha, do you know where Nick usually drinks?' she asks.

'He doesn't. Not much. He might have the occasional drink or two every now and again, but if we ever go to parties or functions or anything he always drives. He doesn't like drinking too much. Not after . . .' I let the words trail off. We both know why Nick doesn't drink much any more.

'But if he does go out, where does he go?' she says, writing in her notebook.

'I don't know. He's been to the Flag a couple of times with friends. I think he quite likes the Old Red Lion, too. Why?'

'What about the Talbot Arms?'

I can't help but let out an involuntary laugh. 'I doubt it. Isn't that place full of drug addicts and benefits cheats?'

Jane McKenna raises an eyebrow. I can't tell whether it's in agreement with me or because of my choice of words about that pub's clientele. 'It's certainly one of the more lively pubs in the town as far as we're concerned. Which is why I was a bit surprised to see Nick going in there earlier today.' She looks at me as if she's expecting me to have some sort of prior knowledge of this. She couldn't be further from the truth.

'I don't know. Why don't you ask him?' I say.

'We would, but we don't know where he is at the moment. We were hoping you might be able to help us with that.'

'Me? If you saw him going in there, then surely you saw where he went after? Are you tailing him or something?'

McKenna gives off a big, beaming, innocent smile. 'No, nothing like that. I just happened to be passing. I was on my way to speak to someone else.' I can tell she's lying.

'And what about the officers who are meant to be keeping an eye on us? On the house? Where were they?'

'They weren't around at that time,' she replies, after a pause. 'We have to be careful where we allocate our resources and we've not had any incidents of press intrusion or anything so we've been scaling things back. But when they're here, they keep an eye on the house, like you say. They can't go following Nick around everywhere. Anyway, why would you want us to be following Nick? You told us you don't suspect him.'

I'm thrown into a daze of confusion by McKenna's words. Press intrusion? Scaling things back? Nick as a suspect? My logical mind knows she's trying to bombard me and squeeze something out of me, and I know she's not allowed to get away with this, but she's come on her own and she's caught me unawares.

'You're meant to be protecting us,' I say, choking back the tears.

'We're trying,' she replies, leaning towards me. 'But first you need to protect yourself.'

37

NICK

Once I'm sitting at Alan's dining room table, I explore a little further. The first thing that occurs to me is that the dark web is a pretty fucked-up place. Alan was right about that. A lot of it I don't understand, but the bits I do I wish I didn't.

The whole set-up of the dark web is very strange. Alan pointed me towards a directory listing of sites, but didn't want anything more to do with it. As I click through the links, I come across what looks like some sort of online marketplace. It's laid out like an old-style message board or image board, the kind which used to be all over the internet in the late nineties. What amazes me is how blatantly the categories are all listed. *Counterfeits, Drug paraphernalia, Drugs, Forgeries, Weapons.* It's astonishing how blatant it all is, as if this is the most normal thing in the world.

It doesn't matter if the authorities see it – and they invariably do all the time – because none of it can be traced. There's no paper trail. No money changing hands – it's all bitcoin and other virtual, untraceable currencies. If the authorities wanted to bust a seller, they couldn't. If they bought off them, they'd just see an anonymous username and that would be it. Sellers could theoretically see who'd bought off them, but the eBay-like feedback system on the marketplace means it'd be almost impossible to buy from a police shill without the police having to sell vast quantities of drugs and weapons beforehand to boost their feedback score. It's almost as if these guys have run across the border and are stood waving at the police, saying *You can't catch us.*

I find a section on the website titled 'Favours in Kind', which seems to list mainly non-financial transactions people are interested in. Most of the language is odd colloquialisms, with obscure references to what seem to mostly be drugs and guns, although there are some posts which are clearly even heavier than that.

I decide to take the plunge and click the 'Register' link. The first thing that hits me is that this is the only website I've ever come across which asks me for only two things: a username and a password. No email address, no name, nothing. I look around the room and try to pick something obscure. I see the drinks cabinet, have no clue what kind of wood it's actually made from, but type *walnut6676* in the username box and choose a password I know I'll remember but which I've never used anywhere else.

That's it. I'm signed up and back in the 'Favours in Kind' section of the website. I take some time to drill down through the locations so I know the advert will be seen by users who are relatively local. Once I get down towards regional and county level, the number of adverts appearing in the section start to dwindle. It seems there aren't too many local people in this part of the marketplace. That's probably a reassuring thing. I don't want to push it too far, so I keep my options open. I'm pretty sure someone'll travel for three grand.

I click the 'New Thread' link and type in the title to my advert, trying to think of a cryptic, underground way to word it. Do I need to? This is the dark web, after all. In the end I plump for *Garbage disposal expert needed. Cash available.* In the text of the advert, I write:

I have need for the removal of a particularly nasty piece of rubbish. Generous cash payment available for experienced and knowledgeable removal expert.

I read it through again. It's cryptic, but not so much that no-one'll know what I'm after. Perhaps just enough to weed out anyone who's not serious. If someone's capable of doing the job for me, they'll know what I'm on about. If, somehow, the authorities were to see it, they'd know, too. Would it be enough to convict me? Possibly, but I'm assured that this is completely untraceable. Besides which, what choice do I have? I need to do this or I'm not going to get Ellie back. With everything piling up on top of me, I have no other option.

I can feel myself starting to get agitated and sense the world closing in around me again, so I try to take a few deep, calm breaths. I have to try and anchor things in normality again. Try to stop my thoughts running away with me. I've got to regain control.

I spend the next hour or so browsing the dark web as well as checking my emails on the internet and generally catching up on some of the stuff I've missed. I try to keep away from the news sites and social media, but I can't help taking a look. I don't delve into the comments sections of any news articles about Ellie, mainly because there aren't many. I don't know whether to be annoyed and upset that the help is dwindling or slightly relieved that it might take off some of the unwanted media attention and allow the police to do their job properly. I guess they're the experts at this sort of thing. If they thought there would be a benefit to keeping the media pressure up, they'd do it. They know what they're doing. And that's what worries me.

When I'm done, I hand the laptop back to Alan and ask if I can use it again as and when needed, just until I've got my own laptop back.

It's always handy to know you've got someone you can count on.

38

NICK

When I get back to the house, Jane McKenna's already there, waiting for me. She smiles at me a little too keenly as I walk into the living room. Tasha seems a little uneasy.

'Hello, Nick,' McKenna says as she finishes drinking her cup of tea. 'I was just updating Natasha on the search. We've had officers combing the woodland out towards the motorway, and the radio appeals are going to go national. It's looking likely that whoever's got Ellie will either be keeping her well hidden or will have taken her further afield by now.'

Well, I could have told you that, I think. In fact, I recall saying as much right from the start. 'So that's it?' I say. 'You've come to give us the news that there's no news?'

'They're doing all they can, Nick,' Tasha says. I wonder why she's suddenly so defensive of the police. It gets to me that she's seemed far more reassured by them than she has been by her own husband. Her reaction to the whole Derek incident and hearing about the Angela thing was kind of understandable, but I still would've expected her to have stood by me a little more firmly. Once again, it feels like Nick against the world. I become even more sure that I'm pursuing the right path to get it all sorted out, once and for all.

'It's fine,' McKenna says, putting a placating hand on Tasha's knee. Seems they've become the best of friends since I went out. 'Actually, Nick, I was just wondering if I could ask you a couple of things.'

Tasha picks up on the subtext quicker than I do. 'I'll go and make some tea.'

'No, it's fine,' I say. 'I'll do it. We can talk in the kitchen.'

I don't think anyone actually even wants tea, so I don't ask. I close the kitchen door behind me and wait to hear what McKenna has to say.

'How have you been coping?' she asks, leaning back against the cupboards, her head cocked slightly to one side.

'About as well as you'd expect, I suppose.'

'Well, I think you're doing a great job. That's the problem, there's not much the parents can do. I guess you feel pretty hopeless and helpless.'

'That about covers it, yeah,' I say.

'I hear you've been getting out and about a bit more over the last day or two.'

Have they been tailing me? 'Yeah, I have. Change of scenery. Bit of fresh air and all that.'

'One of our officers saw you heading into the Talbot Arms,' she says, catching me off guard. I'm pretty sure she sees my eyes flicker. Bitch.

'Really? Oh yeah, I popped in for a quick drink. Trying to take my mind off things, you know. Like you say, there's not much we can do and I just feel like I'm sitting around waiting for news. I'll go stir-crazy.'

'I can imagine,' she says, smiling. 'An odd place to choose, though, isn't it? I mean, it's the other side of town from here.'

'I was passing,' I say, before I can even stop myself. What if the police officer had followed me all the way? They'd know that was bullshit. 'Not somewhere I usually drink, but I didn't really want to go somewhere familiar. I wanted the escapism, I guess.'

McKenna nods. 'You've lived in this town a long time, haven't you?'

'All my life,' I say.

She nods again. 'Never had the best reputation, that pub. Must admit, when I was in uniform I used to spend more time breaking up fights in the Talbot than I did doing anything else.'

'Happens to every pub at some point,' I say, forcing a smile.

'Yeah, but more often than not it's there. That place never changes. Never will, I suspect. Which makes me think it's rather an odd place for you to go for a quick pint. I can't imagine the regulars at the Talbot are the sort of people you're keen to hang around with.'

'Like I said, it's a change of scenery. I didn't want to go somewhere where people would know me.'

'Makes sense,' she replies. 'So you don't know anyone who drinks at the Talbot at all?'

I try to look at her for as long as I can get away with, in some sort of attempt to determine whether or not she knows more than she's letting on.

'No, no-one.'

'Glad to hear it,' she says. 'Some very dodgy characters drink in there, you know. The sort of people you'd be better off keeping well away from.'

'Well, I didn't stay for long,' I say.

'I know.' She stares at me for a little longer than is necessary. 'Still, better than drinking at home alone, eh?' She smiles and pushes herself back upright, away from the kitchen cupboards. 'I'll keep you up to date if there's any more news. Keep positive, won't you?'

I watch as she lets herself out, my fists tightening into whitening bundles of flesh. I feel the eyes of the Rosie Ragdoll searing into the back of my head, feeling every last ounce of my mother's disapproval. I turn, reach up and grab the doll, and put it inside the cereal cupboard, quietening the voices in my mind for just a short while.

39

NICK

'What was that all about?' Tasha says, hearing the door close and coming into the kitchen to see me.

'I don't know,' I say. 'I really don't know.'

She puts the kettle on, clearly wanting that cup of tea after all. 'She was acting all weird before you came back, asking strange questions.'

'What sort of questions?' I ask as nonchalantly as I can. I can see Tasha's been crying, but I don't want to say anything. It feels a bit stupid to ask why in the present situation.

'Stuff about where you'd been over the last few days, if you'd told me. She asked about your friends, too.'

'Friends?' I wonder if perhaps I seemed a little eager with that question.

'Yeah. Wanted to know who you saw on a regular basis, things about your social life,' she says, dropping a teabag in each mug.

'Weird,' I say, trying to sound unperturbed. 'What did you say?'

'What could I say? Only that you don't really go out all that much. Don't really see anyone regularly.'

This unsettles me a bit. I know she's telling the truth, but hearing it makes me a little uneasy. She's right – I've pretty much abandoned most of my friends in the quest for a happy family life. Funny thing is, it hasn't even worked. My daughter's been kidnapped by some psychopath and I'm trying to think of ways to murder my wife. Happy families.

'What did she want to say to you?' Tasha asks, pouring boiling water on the teabags.

'Oh, apparently one of her officers saw me popping into a pub,' I say. The first rule of lying is to tell the absolute truth right up to the bit you don't want the other person to know. That way, you've got less bullshit to remember and stick to. 'I had to get out for a bit and I went over the other side of town for a change of scenery. She thought it was a bit odd, which I suppose it was, so wanted to know why I was there.'

'Christ, what business is it of hers?' Tasha asks. I'm unsure as to whether she's being serious or if she's playing the same game as McKenna.

First rule of lying again. 'Well, I suppose she's going to have her suspicions. Whichever way you look at it, on paper I've got to be their prime suspect. Statistically speaking, one or both of the parents are usually involved when it comes to kids disappearing like this.'

'Don't look at me,' she replies, without even bothering to see if I'm looking at her. 'I was on my way to work. I've got an alibi.' Again, I don't know if she's doing it on purpose or if she's just completely oblivious to her subtext.

'Alibi?' I ask. 'What do you mean, alibi? You're starting to sound like you're in a police interview.'

'Don't start, Nick,' she says. 'You know damn well what I meant.'

'Yeah. Well, I thought I had one until that fucker over the road decided to lie to the police.'

'Why would he do that, Nick?' Tasha asks, turning to face me with one hand on her hip. Now I know she's more than aware of what she's doing.

'I don't know. I really don't know. I've been trying to think of what I could possibly have done to upset him, but I just can't. I mean, I guess it's possible that he didn't see anything, but I can't imagine for one second that the day Ellie went missing was the first day he hadn't been spying out of his window.'

'Do you really think he's involved somehow?' Tasha says after a few seconds' silence.

'I hope not,' I reply. 'I dunno. Yeah, he's a bit weird, but if he was a child abductor don't you think something would've been done by now? Like McKenna said, his record's clean. Yes, unlike mine, before you say it.'

'I wasn't going to,' she lies.

There's a good twenty seconds or so of complete silence, in which I decide to root around in the cupboards for a biscuit. What's left unsaid is louder than anything that could be spoken, and I'll be damned if I'm going to be the first one to say anything.

40

NICK

I don't fancy another day of moping around the house, but I do want to see if my post on the dark web has had any replies, so I decide to head round to Alan's. McKenna will know – somehow – but I don't think it'd be unreasonable to argue that even the most unsociable of people would want to seek comfort in the arms of friends when their daughter has gone missing.

When I get to Alan's, I see he's left the laptop on the same spot on the dining table, untouched. This doesn't surprise me; Alan's a trustworthy kind of guy, and he's not the sort of person to get much use out of his dining table, anyway, judging by the empty drinks cans and ready-meal packages stacked up on his kitchen work surface.

I open the laptop and wait for it to boot up before loading the Tor browser and navigating my way to the site. It seems to take an age, but I know I'm just being impatient. I log in and see a *(1)* next to my username. I presume this is the number of responses I've had. Better than nothing, though. I click the *(1)* and the response pops up on the screen.

> *How much are we talking? Depends on type of rubbish and disposal method you want. We can talk.*

Cagey, but promising. I click 'Reply' and quickly type out a response.

> *Three grand. Can't negotiate – that's literally all I have. Method up to you, whatever's quickest. Will provide details later, but it's a light load.*

It seems bizarre that we're both keeping it so cryptic, considering the secrecy and anonymity of the dark web, but I'm not complaining. So far as I can see, there's absolutely nothing incriminating so far. Sure, a copper with even half an ounce of common sense would know what it was all about, but there's nothing whatsoever that would stand up in a court. Besides, the anonymity is keeping me extra safe for now.

The anonymity is something that'll have to be broken, though. As soon as I identify Tasha as the target, the odds will be stacked against me in terms of the killer working out who I am. I can throw him off that trail, though, by telling him I'm someone else and she tucked me up over a business deal. There's nothing to trace it back to me. Not if I'm careful.

There's a deep-seated worry that this person might not even be genuine. What's to say they're not just going to take my three grand and disappear? How do I know they're actually going to go through with it? What if it's a police sting?

I shake that last thought from my head. It's impossible. I was the one who initiated the whole thing. But how do I know this person is trustworthy? I don't know who he is or have any sort of guarantee it's going to happen, but what choice do I have? If I want the reassurance of Warren's word, it's going to cost me an extra twelve grand that I don't have. Besides which, I'm not about to draw up a fucking contract with some anonymous hitman I found on the internet. These things are all about trust. They have to be. A gentleman's agreement. His word is his bond.

Handing over the money could be tricky, so I'd have to arrange some sort of dead drop. I'd leave the cash hidden in a container, somewhere no-one else will find it, then send him a dark web message telling him where it is. As long as I keep well away from cameras while I'm doing it and make sure the money's put somewhere it can't be accidentally found by someone else, I should be in the clear.

By the time I've pondered all this, I've already got a response waiting for me. This guy's keen.

> *That's cheap, but doable. Won't be anything fancy, though. Low risk method needed. Identify the target and I'll see if it can be done.*

Christ. *Identify the target.* This is sounding almost military. I guess that means he'll be efficient.

I realise that he's probably going to want a photo of Tasha. How am I supposed to get one of those to him? I can't go putting one on a computer without being traced. I'm going to need to think this through carefully.

I lean back in the chair and think. Whatever it is, it's going to need to look natural. As natural as someone dying can look. Nothing too obvious like a shooting, but then again trying to make it look like suicide has its own risks, too. No, it needs to look accidental.

I remember the idea I had a little while back. What about a mugging gone wrong? Tasha's so bloody obstinate, if some bloke tried to mug her or nick her bag she's just the sort of person who'd try to argue and fight back and end up getting herself seriously hurt or worse. *Or worse.*

But where? She rarely goes out without me, and I sure as hell need to make sure I'm nowhere near when it happens, as I'm going to need the alibi. It'll need to be done somewhere that won't be too busy and preferably not in broad daylight, either. Fortunately for me, Tasha's pretty fearless so she's not the sort of person who'd walk the long way round just to stick to main roads.

I think back to my meeting with Mark in Jubilee Park. Almost no-one walks through Jubilee Park at night, even though it's completely open. Tasha has a friend, Emma, who lives on the other side of Jubilee Park. She'd need to walk – no, *would* walk – through the park to get to Emma's house. I'd really rather not involve Emma, though, if I can help it. She's not the sort of person I'd really want to spend too much time with, but Tash has managed to systematically alienate every single one of her other friends. Even Cristina and Leanne aren't massively keen on her. Before I know it, I've got my phone out of my pocket and I'm calling Emma.

'Nick, good to hear from you,' she says. A blatant lie. She's been weird with me for years. 'How are things? I mean, apart from the obvious. Is there any news?'

'No, nothing really. All we can do is wait. There's nothing much else we can do. That's the hardest part,' I say. Sympathy vote, please. 'It's starting to get to us both a bit, if I'm honest. Tasha says she's alright, but I know her. She's struggling as much as any of us. That's why I'm ringing, actually. She won't say anything, but I think she needs a friend.'

'Oh?'

'Yeah. Don't tell her I told you this, though. You know what she's like.' I let out a small chuckle, trying to loosen the atmosphere. 'I was thinking perhaps if you called her and invited her over to your place tomorrow night, I think that'd help her a lot. Help take her mind off things and give her some support, change of scenery, y'know. Get a few of the girls together and try to get her to relax.'

There's a pause before she speaks. 'Yeah, course,' she says. 'I'll do whatever I can. Must be hard just waiting for news. You must feel helpless.'

'We do,' I say.

'No worries, I'll give her a call now.' There's a short pause before she speaks again. 'And how are you bearing up, Nick?'

'I've had better times,' I say, trying to shrug it off. 'Oh, and Emma? Can you do me one huge favour?'

There's a short pause before she replies. 'Of course. What is it?'

'Don't tell anyone that I suggested this. Especially not Tasha. You know what she's like if she thinks people are trying to mollycoddle her.'

I can almost hear Emma smiling at the other end of the phone. 'Of course.'

Once the rest of the updates and pleasantries are out of the way and the phone is back in my pocket, I realise how quickly things have moved. I click 'Reply' on the dark web site and update the stranger.

> *It'll be tomorrow night, Jubilee Park. Needs to look accidental. Cash will be ready by then. Description to come.*

I hear Alan shuffling around upstairs and I find myself letting out a small yelp. I know I've got to stay calm. Getting jumpy isn't going to do me any favours.

A few seconds later, another message pings through on the laptop.

> *That's not much notice. Will need closer contact. Have throwaway mob: 07700919663. Geoff.*

Geoff. Is that his real name? I'm guessing not.

He might well have a throwaway mobile, but I certainly don't. Can withheld numbers be traced by police if they need to? I don't know, but I can't risk it. I'm going to have to use phone boxes, and then preferably ones without CCTV anywhere nearby. I wouldn't know where to get a throwaway mobile of my own, and was under the impression that even pay-as-you-go SIMs had to be registered to a name and address nowadays. The phone box seems like the only option.

I decide I need to head home and be with Tash. Once she's been invited over to Emma's, she'll let me know the times and I can call Geoff to update him.

I intend to leave the cash in a holdall, hidden in the woods outside the town. There's a small copse out towards Huish Farm which is pretty dense and has thick undergrowth and piles of old leaves. I go out walking there quite a lot when I need to clear my head or work through a particular plot point in my books. Tasha and I sometimes take Ellie for walks around there when the weather's good, but that's rare. We used to do it far more often, but nowadays I just find myself walking in the woods on my own instead. Story of my life.

I'll bury the holdall under the leaves in the undergrowth in the woods, which'll be fine for a few hours or a day or two. In fact, you could probably leave it there for months and no-one would find it. Aside from the odd dog walker or two, it's not exactly a busy thoroughfare.

I stand back and think for a moment. This is becoming real. I'm actually making plans and coming up with hiding places, routes and excuses. It scares me a little. It's somewhat too real, too vivid. And it's at that point that I realise I'm actually going to have to go through with this after all.

All of a sudden, things are moving very quickly.

41

NICK

When I get back home, I find a note from Tash to say she's popped out for an hour to get some shopping. I always feel a pang of guilt when I see signs of normality like this. When a child goes missing, your life stops dead, yet there are things which have to continue as normal, like eating and sleeping. That's one of the worst things about it; feeling guilty for carrying out your natural bodily functions. That's what it does to you.

I'm glad Tash isn't here as I need to get the money from the safe and go. Doing that with her in the house would be more than difficult. I have a sudden bolt of adrenaline as I realise how woefully unprepared I am for this. It was meant to be a carefully thought-through plan, but now I seem to be racing along at a hundred miles an hour, thinking of things just as I'm doing them. This worries me.

Ever since I received the photo of Ellie, I've known I needed to do something quickly. I'd known before that, but not as definitely. Seeing her little face was heartbreaking, and right now I'm battling between the side of me that desperately wants her back and the side that knows I need to remain calm and collected if this is to work.

Then again, you've got to take your chances.

I sprint up the stairs and into the bedroom, where I open the safe. The cash is still there. I open my wardrobe, remove my sports bag and put the cash inside. It's an awkward amount – far too much to fit in a pocket or jacket, but lost inside my sports bag. To make it look less suspicious, I grab a towel and a pair of trainers from the wardrobe and throw them in, too.

I realise that I'm going to have to take the car. I've not wanted to use it up until now – not for anything other than the usual stuff – as part of me is convinced they've put some sort of tracker on it. My logical mind tells me they can't have done, though. They'd need to get a warrant to do that, and that means they'd need sufficient evidence that I was involved in Ellie's disappearance. Besides which, there's just no real way of me getting to the woods without my car. If the worst comes to worst and they find out I was there, I'll tell them I decided not to go to the gym and opted for a run around the woods in the fresh air instead.

I know that if I stop I'll change my mind, and I know I can't change my mind. I need to stick to the plan. I need Ellie back.

I head back downstairs and out the front door, which is when I see McKenna walking up the front path with a carrier bag in each hand. Tasha's walking behind her.

'Hi, Nick. Off somewhere?' McKenna says.

'To the gym,' I say, holding up the sports bag. 'I need to blow off some steam.'

'Must be difficult sitting around waiting for news,' she says. 'Not knowing what's happened.'

'Yeah, it is. Just makes us feel so helpless, y'know? Frustrating. Which is why,' I say, walking towards my car, 'I'm off to pound the treadmill.'

'Enjoy,' McKenna replies, looking at me for a little longer than feels comfortable before heading into the house. Tasha stops to speak to me.

'Before I forget, Emma called while I was out. She's asked me if I want to go over to her place tomorrow night with Leanne and Cristina. Thinks it might do me good to get out of the house.'

'She's probably right. There's nothing much we can do other than go mad waiting. Distractions help,' I say, holding up the sports bag again.

'I know. But it still feels wrong somehow. If I do decide to go, it'll be at about eight, so I won't be back late,' she replies, leaning across to kiss me on the cheek as she walks past and into the house.

'Have fun at the gym,' McKenna says from the doorway, having already put the bags in the kitchen. I start up my car and drive off down the road.

I keep one eye on my rear-view mirror as I head off towards the town centre before turning up a side road and heading in the direction of the woods. I'm careful to make sure no-one's following me, as I'd find it pretty tricky to explain why I'm heading for the woods with a sports bag.

The wooded area isn't accessible by car, so I park up in a nearby road next to some houses, making sure the car doesn't stand out like a sore thumb, and I walk up the footpath and through the field to the copse.

Fortunately, I see no-one on my way. The weather's not ideal for dog walkers or families out exploring. When I reach the copse, I stick to the well-worn path for a few yards before checking around me and veering off between the trees, my feet stumbling as I try to traverse the logs and thickets to get deeper into the undergrowth.

Once I'm satisfied there's no-one here, I use my boot to scrape aside a pile of leaves and dead branches and plonk the bag down on the damp mud before covering it back over. How I'm going to describe where this is, I don't know. I scurry around in the leaves to find a sharp stone. I find something which looks a bit like flint, and I leave a mark on the nearest tree – an *X*. I retrace my steps back to the path and draw an arrow on a tree, pointing in the direction of the bag. It's not obvious to anyone casually walking past, but visible enough to someone looking for it.

Even though I know it's well hidden, I feel pretty uneasy just leaving three grand in a bag in the middle of the woods. Not as uneasy as I feel about coming face-to-face with the man who's going to kill my wife, though, or having to identify myself to give it to him directly. I can handle losing three grand if that's the alternative.

I retrace my steps back across the field to my car. I know there's a phone box in the next village, Medbury – one which won't have CCTV cameras anywhere near it. To be honest, I'd be surprised if Medbury had electricity. I start up the car and head in the direction of the village.

When I get there, I decide to leave my car a hundred yards or so away from the phone box. I'm not entirely sure why, but it just seems to feel safer. I get out and walk to the payphone, trying not to look too suspicious as I glance around me. I fish the piece of paper with Geoff's number on it out of my pocket before lifting the receiver and dialling. I drop a pound coin in the slot as he answers.

'Yeah?'

'Geoff?' I ask. It's all I can think of to say.

'Yeah,' he replies.

'It's the guy who wanted the removal job done,' I say.

'I know who you are. I don't reuse SIM cards,' he says. That both reassures me and puts me on edge. He seems like a serious, professional kind of guy.

'Oh, okay. Good,' I reply. 'If you head to the woods by Huish Farm, just outside Medbury, there are signs for a public bridleway. Follow the path into the woods. You'll see a tree on your left. That'll get you to where you need to be.' I try to keep it as vague as I can, not mentioning money or anything of the sort. I guess you can never be too careful.

'Right. And what about the job?' he asks, a man of few words.

'Female, mid thirties. She'll be walking east through Jubilee Park between eight and quarter past, wearing a cream-coloured coat with a fur-lined hood.' It's the only way I can think of to describe Tasha. I have no idea what she'll be wearing and there's no way I can try to dictate that to her, but I know which coat she'll be wearing – the one she always wears.

'Any preference on method?'

'Something quick, but needs to look accidental.'

'Will she be carrying a bag? Phone? Money?' he asks.

'Yes, all of them I should think.'

'Right. Mugging gone wrong, then,' he says.

It sounds daft saying it to a contract killer, but I start speaking before I've even realised. 'Be careful, though,' I say. 'She's pretty feisty. She'll probably try fighting back.'

'Oh, I'm not worried about that,' he says. 'Is that all I need to know?'

'Uh, yeah,' I reply. What else is there to say? This isn't exactly something I tend to do every day.

'Good. If the money's where you say it is, we're on. Either way, don't call this number again.'

Before I can say anything, he's hung up the phone. A lump forms in my throat as I now realise this whole thing is completely irreversible.

42

TASHA

'What a time to go to the gym,' Jane says as I take the tins from the carrier bags and put them into the cupboards. Her presence here has become completely normal recently. She's almost a part of the family.

'Yeah, well, that's Nick for you,' I say, not wanting to add anything else.

'Maybe he wants to get rid of his frustrations through exercise. Wear himself out.'

'Maybe,' I reply.

'His way of having some normality. Something to take his mind off things, perhaps.'

I put a tin down on the shelf in the cupboard a little harder than I normally would. 'Perhaps.' I think she senses I'm uncomfortable, as she quickly changes the subject.

'I swear they're making these carrier bags thinner nowadays. Bit of a con, really, seeing as they charge us 5p for each one.'

'Got to look after the environment,' I say, in a flat tone.

'True, but it's not doing the environment much good if I have to use three times as many bags because they've made them twice as thin.'

I let out a small sigh, my hand resting on a tin of beans. I don't lift it. I just stand, staring at the tiles on the wall. 'No, I suppose not.'

Jane doesn't say anything for a few moments, but I can tell she's looking at me. I hear her intake of breath before she speaks to me in her faux-casual way again.

'Does Nick go to the gym often, then?'

'Not very often, no,' I reply, my voice almost a whisper.

'Which one's he a member of?'

I swallow. 'I don't know.'

'You don't know?' Her voice doesn't sound particularly shocked. It's almost as if she expected me to say it. Of course she did. She knows already. She's just trying to get me to say it. 'Surely you know which gym he goes to. Unless he goes to more than one.'

'He has done,' I say. 'I think he just does a pay-as-you-go thing now. Bit silly paying every month if you don't go that often.'

'That's true,' Jane replies, her tone becoming much more friendly again. 'In fact, I think I remember seeing an article once about why it's pointless doing exercise at all unless it's regular. Otherwise you just cycle. A bit like yo-yo dieting. You need to keep it up. It's all about lifestyle changes. Sometimes you need to make big changes and sacrifices in order to get what you really want. It's not always easy, but sometimes you need to do it.'

I can't help myself. 'Are we still talking about Nick's non-existent exercise regime or are you trying to get at something else?' I bark.

Jane looks genuinely shocked that I've snapped. 'No. Like what? I was just asking because neither of you have ever mentioned the gym before and it seemed a bit odd that he was suddenly off there at the moment. Especially seeing as I had enough trouble getting you out of the house to get some basic groceries.'

'Yeah, well, we're all different. Nick likes to get out of the house and distract himself. I don't.'

'Maybe you should think about it,' she says, coming over behind me and placing a calming hand on my shoulder. 'You shouldn't feel guilty about living. You can't beat yourself up over things and sit stewing, because it won't make things any better. It won't affect the odds of Ellie coming home. But it does mean that when she comes home her parents won't have turned into complete nut jobs.' She says this with a small chuckle, trying to lighten the mood. It doesn't work. 'Come on,' she says, shaking my shoulder slightly. 'Leave the worrying to us, eh? We get paid for it. Not nearly enough, but still.'

'I don't know,' I say, wresting myself free from her grip. 'It still doesn't feel right going over to Emma's for wine when my daughter's missing. It's perverse.'

'More perverse than sitting in your darkened living room staring at the walls?' she asks. 'It'll do you good to be around friends. To have a change of scenery. I'll know where you are if I need to get hold of you, and I imagine Nick'll be here, anyway. If he's not off down the gym or his new favourite pub again.'

Just as I'm about to agree with her, her tone makes me reconsider. I really don't like the way she's speaking about Nick. It's not that I don't have my own worries about him, because I do, but the way she's saying things makes him sound like a criminal. He's not a criminal; he's just useless and naïve. He always has been, but this time it feels like he's trying to cover something up. A large part of me hopes it's just because he feels guilty about going back inside the house and leaving Ellie in the car. Another part of me doesn't want him to feel guilty, but I can't help but blame him for a huge part of it. 'You don't need to say things like that,' I tell Jane. 'Nick's not a bad person.'

She nods. 'I know that. He's dealing with things his way, and you need to deal with things your way. I just think that some distraction for a couple of hours probably wouldn't hurt.'

'But it feels wrong,' I say. 'I feel as though I'm letting Ellie down by not being here.'

Jane puts her hand back on my shoulder again. 'You aren't. Trust me. You do whatever you feel comfortable with, but I can promise you that nobody will think any less of you for wanting to get out and clear your head for an hour or two. Ellie certainly wouldn't.'

I think for a few moments, then nod my head.

43

NICK

I sat in my car for longer than was natural, but it felt right. I couldn't rush home as I needed to be out for an hour and a half or so – just in case McKenna was there again when I got home.

A thought crosses my mind. Would she want to check out all the local gyms to see if I was a member? Some were pay-as-you-go, but would she then want to know which one I'd been to and check up on me? I try to push the thought from my mind as I realise that I'll be going home without my sports bag, too.

What explanation am I going to come up with? *I decided not to go to the gym in the end, and just drove for a bit* is pretty plausible considering the situation we're in. *I lost my bag, too* is probably pushing it. It feels mad having to explain something so seemingly unimportant, but in the eyes of the police I'm suspect number one and that's only going to get a hell of a lot worse as the next couple of days pan out.

I guess I could say I left it at the gym. Perhaps I didn't work up much of a sweat – couldn't get myself motivated – so I decided that it'd be easier to just leave my stuff in a locker until the next time. That all sounds great until they want to know which gym I was at so they can check up.

Will they want to check up, though? Could I feasibly tell them to mind their own business? Things will change after tomorrow. Not cooperating with the police when my daughter's gone missing and my wife's just been killed isn't going to look all that good. I guess my only option is to get another sports bag and put it in a locker at a gym. Can't be too careful.

The drive back seems longer than I had expected. Time appears to have slowed. I wonder if my brain has warped its perception of the passing of time to try and allow it to process the thousands of thoughts and emotions going through it.

When I get home, I'm relieved to find that McKenna isn't there. I know we're meant to feel reassured by the police presence, but for some reason McKenna makes me feel uneasy. I know that I've not exactly done myself any favours in their eyes over the past few days. But I still can't shake that horrible sense of injustice that they seem to be concentrating more on trying to catch me out or make me feel uneasy than they are on trying to find Ellie.

That's unfair on them. I know it is. I know they'll be doing all they can to find her and that it's not an easy job, but that instinctive, primal sense of desperation at wanting your child safe and with you is something only a parent will ever understand.

I'm finding it hard to look at Tasha. She's there when I get back, and it's impossible to describe the feeling I have towards her. It's almost completely empty. It sounds so strange to be so matter-of-fact about it, but I think my brain has already accepted the fact that she won't be around much longer. It feels strange saying that after so long together, but I've really not been happy in the relationship. I don't know how long I've felt like that, but I can only imagine it must have been years. Why else would I feel absolutely nothing, knowing that tomorrow night she'll be dead? Maybe it's because it pales into insignificance in my mind compared to the possibility that Ellie might come to some harm.

I start to wonder what might have happened if we'd never been put in this situation. Would we just have carried on as normal, me continuing to be unhappy in the marriage? Or would we have eventually drifted apart and got divorced? What effect would that have had on Ellie? They say the divorce of parents can have a hugely detrimental effect on children. I wouldn't want that for Ellie.

That's not to say that the death of a parent wouldn't have the same effect, of course, but at least there's some closure there. With a divorce there's always a permanent reminder. The flitting between two houses, weekly schedules, visitation orders, deciding who's going where for Christmas and birthdays . . . At least death is final. You can move on.

I don't know why I'm trying to justify myself. There's no justification needed. I just want Ellie back.

Tasha's sitting at the kitchen table, browsing through Facebook. Personally, I don't see the point. I've got more than enough going on in my own life right now without having to find out what someone I went to school with had for lunch.

'Everything alright?' I ask. Ever the dutiful husband.

'Just trying to take my mind off things,' she says, emotionless. 'How was the gym?'

'Not great. Couldn't get motivated,' I say, sticking to the plan. 'I feel bad just sitting around here waiting for news, but I feel guilty doing something else instead.'

Tasha just nods. I notice that she's stopped scrolling down the page. She doesn't appear to be reading anything, either. I stand beside the table and notice a stray tear running down her cheek. I put a reassuring arm around her.

'They'll find her,' I say. Tasha throws her arms around me and sobs heavily onto my shoulder. She's clinging on to me like a mountain climber who's lost his harness.

'Nick, I'm so scared,' she cries through fitful sobs.

'I know, honey, I know. But they'll find her. I know they will.'

'What if they don't? What if . . . What if she's dead?' Now she's looking me in the eye, willing me to say something.

'She isn't. I can tell. I can feel it,' I say, knowing I can say this with a fair amount of certainty. Tasha seems to pick up on my confidence, and it looks as though it's given her some sort of reassurance.

'Thank you,' she says, almost a whisper. 'I love you, Nick.'

She looks pained, broken. And all of a sudden I'm feeling very, very unsure of myself.

44

TASHA

I sit staring at the wall, silently cursing myself for having not said anything. I'd had it all planned. I was going to wait until he got home and confront him about the gym thing. I was going to ask him which gym he went to, why he'd suddenly decided he wanted to go now and, ultimately, what he'd really been up to. But I bottled it.

I knew deep down that he hadn't gone to the gym. He never goes to the gym. Not in the past few years, anyway. Sure, he's had memberships like everyone else, but he cancelled the last one a good two years ago after letting it run for a while. He's never particularly been a fitness freak, and he's lucky that his general physique and metabolism mean that he doesn't need to be. But that's not all that led me to think that there was no way he'd been at the gym. After the events of the past few days, and with the benefit of hindsight, I now realise that I can tell when my husband's keeping something from me. I know when he's lying.

I think I've always known, but I didn't want to admit to it. I knew there was something in Nick's past that I wouldn't want to know about, and I think I was protecting myself by not probing any further or even allowing myself to think about it. Maybe it was a defence mechanism. Maybe it was selfishness. Or maybe it was because I'd been blinded by love. I know it's likely a combination of all three, but that third possibility made me wonder whether the implication then is that I don't love Nick any more. Can something like what we've been through really cause couples to fall apart that easily? Sure, we're far from what most people might consider the perfect couple, and before Ellie was born I was certain we'd drift away from each other, but she provided the glue that we needed. She's what was missing. And now that she's gone, what else do we have to hold us together? A web of lies.

Even though I knew Nick hadn't been at the gym and was planning to confront him about it, when he turned up without his gym bag it threw me. Totally threw me. I was expecting he'd at least come back with the bag, perhaps a towel over his shoulder, splashed a bit of water on his face to look sweaty. But there was nothing. Almost as if he was blatantly throwing it in my face that he'd been lying to me at the same time as assuming I was stupid enough to fall for it.

And that's when I realised that everything was falling apart. It sounds daft to hear myself say it, but what sort of relationship is it when you can't even be bothered to lie convincingly to your partner? When there's such contempt in the air that you don't go to the effort of creating a convincing backstory? Maybe he needs his space. Maybe he wanted a cover so he could go out and buy me a present. Building secrecy doesn't mean he's up to something.

With Nick strolling into the house and into the kitchen as if nothing had happened, I didn't know what to do or think. All of those thoughts came into my head at once, but the one which trumped them all was an unshakeable feeling of pity. I think I'm over feeling sorry for myself. I think Jane's words made sense. And in that moment I saw Nick out of the corner of my eye and I felt sorry for him. That he'd tried to conceal where he was going and not even been in a state to do it properly. That he felt he had to lie to me in the first place. That this whole situation is dragging us apart. Ellie, our precious daughter, who kept us together in the first place, has started to create huge fissures in our relationship without even knowing about it. It's not her fault, of course it's not. It's our fault and no-one's fault at the same time. It's the fault of whoever's taken her. The nameless person we don't know. The thing we can't do anything about. And in that moment I just felt so helpless.

I regret not saying anything. The moment was so fleeting, so intense, that I couldn't do anything but struggle to hold back the tears. Everything came at once. And now the moment is gone. It doesn't feel right questioning Nick now. I don't need to know. When he held me and told me that he knew in his heart that Ellie would be fine, I could see that in his eyes. I knew he believed it. It's hard to describe, but when you really know somebody you can tell a lot just by looking into their eyes. You can see sincerity, determination, passion. And I saw all of those things when he told me that he knew Ellie would be fine. It wasn't just hope – it was a deep-seated, unshakeable belief. In that split second, everything changed. When I told him I loved him, I meant it. Right from that moment, from that look in his eyes, I felt like I had my husband back.

45

NICK

I was awake for most of last night. Tasha opening up to me had thrown me somewhat. She'd always been cold and aloof, but last night I saw a different side to her. I saw her vulnerability, her pained soul. And I saw a different side to myself, too. I saw my conscience.

In any other marriage, it would have been a beautiful, poignant moment. It would've been in this marriage, too, had it not come at this point. I tried telling myself that I was just being tested, that I couldn't possibly fall for it. I had to stick with the plan, no matter what. After all, it was the only way I was ever going to get Ellie back.

But try as I might, I couldn't quite get over the fact that I actually felt something last night. Something new.

The morning has gone slowly. Tasha's been out with the police on their searches. They've been scouring the local fields and woodland – fortunately for me, nowhere near Medbury. She said she had to at least feel as though she was doing something. It's been a bit of a blessing for me, because although I'm just sitting at home by the phone, waiting for news I know isn't going to come, at least I've been left alone by the journalists. They're all out trying to get the exclusive shot of Tasha joining the police in the search for Ellie.

The worst thing about the silence and loneliness is that it leaves you to think. I spent all night thinking, and right now I just want to be able to sleep. Even leaning back in the enveloping armchair, deprived of sleep and in the company of only the ticking clock on the mantelpiece, I'm still unable to stop the express train of thoughts and doubts running through my mind.

I'd always heard people saying that these sorts of situations are both physically and mentally draining. I'd never really understood how extreme stress could make you physically tired, but now I do. I'm more than tired; I'm exhausted. I feel like I've been through twelve rounds with Mike Tyson.

And this is all bearing in mind that I know Ellie will be safe. That she'll be coming home very soon. How must Tasha feel, with the added uncertainty?

Now that everything's arranged, I need only wait for time. I'm trying to force through logical, coherent thoughts. I try to focus on the positives. Ellie will be home soon. This will all be over. Tasha will be gone. It'll be Ellie and her daddy. Just the two of us.

I'm still numb about the whole thing. Should I not be feeling something more? I wonder if perhaps my writing has numbed me. Can reading and writing about murder and death make it all seem completely normal? It seems bizarre that one could ever become so completely desensitised to death, but I suppose it's possible.

As the day continues, I start to philosophise more and more. I realise I'm starting to get political and philosophical about the whole situation. Is it right to take a life to save a life? What if the lives are the wife you no longer love – or even like – and the daughter you love desperately?

When it comes down to the simple point of having to choose one to die and one to live, there's no choice to be made.

But I still can't shake the nagging feeling at the back of my mind. If I'm so sure of myself and my decision, why am I analysing it constantly? Why can I not just let the decision go and look forward to the fact that in just a few hours I'll have Ellie back?

How will she return? Will she just be left on the driveway in the same manner in which she was taken? How will the kidnapper do that without being seen? What will Ellie say?

I have a thought. I'm pretty sure she must have seen her kidnapper and will be able to describe where she's been since she was taken. The kidnapper will know this, too. Ellie's a smart girl. You only need to spend a few minutes with her to realise that. The kidnapper will sure as hell have spotted it. They'd be identified sooner or later.

I feel my heart leap in my chest as this hits me. What if that was the intention the whole time? What if they never let Ellie go? What if this whole plan was to have Tasha killed and then ensure they could never be found by keeping hold of Ellie – or worse? If they're the sort of person who can kidnap a young girl and demand a husband murder his wife, what's to say they won't kill Ellie, too?

I'm jolted out of my thought process by Tasha arriving home. She tells me she's going to shower, change and head out to Emma's. The whole day has disappeared in a blur, and all of a sudden I realise this is about to happen. It's actually going ahead. Within minutes, Tasha will come downstairs and head out the door and it'll be the last time I ever see her until I have to identify her body on a mortuary slab.

I pace the room, alternating between blind panic and trying to assure myself that I've made a decision and I need to stick to it. Last-minute nerves are understandable.

The time goes quickly and Tasha comes into the living room to say goodbye. I try to act normally, push it all to the back of my mind. Out of sight, out of mind. When I hear the latch on the front door click and her heels clip-clopping down the driveway, I panic.

I run into the kitchen and pick up the phone. I know it's not wise to use my own phone, but right now I don't care. It's got to be done. I dial the number, my hands shaking as I try not to press the wrong buttons. After what seems like an age, it rings.

'Yeah?' comes the answer, eventually.

'Geoff? There's been a change of plan,' I say. 'Can you—'

He cuts me off before I can say anything. 'I told you not to call. It's too risky,' he says.

'I know, but—'

'No buts,' he replies, interrupting me again. Before I can say another word, he's disconnected the call. I swear and call back. It goes straight through to answerphone. I try again, twice, three times, four times. He's switched his phone off.

I run upstairs and grab a pair of shoes, cramming my feet into them and rushing to tie up the shoelaces. It takes twice as long as it usually does, my hands shaking and fingers not doing what I want them to. I take the stairs two at a time and head out the front door, slamming it behind me. I have to stop this. Now.

When I get to the end of my drive, I see Derek putting the rubbish out in his bin. He stops at the same time I do and we look at each other. After a few seconds I glance off down the road in the direction of Jubilee Park. I can't see Tasha.

I look back at Derek. He's still looking at me. In a rare moment of clarity, I realise I have to stay. This is my alibi.

46

TASHA

A huge part of me feels guilty about tonight. I mean, who the hell goes round to their friend's house for drinks when their five-year-old daughter is missing? But then I remember that Nick's right. There's nothing we can do at this stage other than sit at home and allow ourselves to get sucked into worrying about the worst that could have happened. What good would that do us?

We can't do anything. The police are doing the best they can, and although I've got to admit I'm getting really frustrated at how slowly it all seems to be moving, even they've advised us to try and maintain as much normality as we can. The problem is, I can't remember what normality really is. Everything before is a blur: days at work, holidays, trips to the park. All jumbled into one. I would say it's the medication doing it, but I know it isn't. I know it's the trauma. It's what happens when you go through something like this. Everything becomes either Before or After.

I'm putting on a brave face, I know, but I'm doing it for both of us. I'm doing it because right now Nick is all I have. And that worries me. I know he's not coping. I don't blame him. Who could? But Nick starts to act strangely when he's struggling. He's never been one to cope well with difficult situations, but his behaviour's been worrying me more and more.

I don't know if it's just that I'm looking too far into things, but before (there's that word again), I doubt whether I would've had Nick down as someone who'd encourage me to go round to Emma's for a bottle of wine while our daughter is missing. He resented me going back to work after she was born, so it seems highly unlikely.

Regardless, I think we could do with a few hours apart. We've started to get under each other's feet even more than usual, and things have almost blown up a couple of times. Deep down, I can't help but feel as though I need to blame him for what's happened to Ellie. What if he hadn't gone back in the house that morning? What if he'd actually got himself organised for once in his life and had taken Ellie to school at the time he was meant to? What if he'd just manned up and told Ellie she'd have to take the picture of Miss Williams in another day? And then I begin to turn it on myself. What if I hadn't had to go to this conference? What if I'd gone in later and actually stepped up to the plate as a mother and got Ellie ready for school myself? The whole thing's full of *what ifs*, and it's not doing us any good.

I'm not trying to distract myself from what's happening, but I am trying to stop myself from going over old ground and slowly killing myself with resentment and regret. I know in my heart of hearts that Ellie will be brought back to us. Call it hope. Call it desperation. But every fibre of my being holds on for that moment Ellie comes home. And when she does, I want her to be back home the way things were, not in a house full of bad feelings and negative atmosphere.

And then I feel guilty for feeling like that. As if I'm almost duty-bound to be pacing around the house and pulling my hair out, as if I'm a bad mother for not screaming in hysterics on the floor. Does Nick think that of me? And what of the police? I'm presuming they've already checked CCTV at the train station. Part of me hopes they have so that they can see I was nowhere near the house when Ellie went missing, and another part of me hopes they haven't as that would mean they've actually suspected me of kidnapping my own daughter.

There's one unshakeable contradiction that I don't want to face, but which keeps rearing its ugly head: I'm convinced Ellie is safe and will return home, but at the same time I can't think of anyone who'd specifically want to take her. If that's the case, it only leaves the possibility of an opportunistic kidnapper. And why would an opportunistic kidnapper want to keep her perfectly safe and looked after if they just wanted—

I scrub the thought from my mind. I can't let myself think like that. I've got the same desperate worries and sickening thoughts any mother would have, but I'm also fighting tooth and nail to push them to the back of my mind and maintain as much hope and optimism as I can. But even that's fading quickly.

The medication's taking the edge off of things, but that's not saying much. Without it, I'd be unable to even function. And again I feel guilty for even being able to function. What it has done is slow these thoughts down and allowed me to process them. It's held me back from the edge.

It's a feeling of numbness that takes over as I start to walk through Jubilee Park. As the glow of the streetlights fades behind me, I feel solace and familiarity in the darkness of the park. The blackness of the night and the silence around me feels just like the enormous buffer of reality I'm feeling every day. Seeing people going to work, getting on with their daily lives, probably completely unaware of what's happened. Unaware that the world's stopped turning. I feel like I'm in a bubble, completely removed from reality. Like the park, a black mass surrounded by a dim glow of streetlights, growing ever dimmer.

I'm snapped out of my thoughts by the sound of a single footstep crunching on dead leaves and twigs. Before I can turn my head to look, I sense it filling with pain and the lights flash in front of my eyes, drowning out the orange glow of the streetlights that twist and turn as my cheek hits the tarmac.

47

NICK

Sitting around waiting for news is horrible. I know, because it's what I've spent the past few days doing. Sitting around waiting for bad news is worse, particularly when you know what the news is going to be. I'm just waiting for the call to tell me that Tasha is dead.

It feels weirdly peaceful, tranquil. As if the whole sorry saga is almost over and I'll be reunited with my Ellie. How will Ellie's kidnapper know the deed has been done in order to return her? Do I need to email Jen Hood? That's not something I want to risk. I don't want to incriminate myself any further.

Whoever it is, they didn't have much difficulty in coming very close to us on two separate occasions – when Ellie was taken and when I received the message about the police officer outside the house – so they probably won't have too much trouble doing so again. It's pretty likely that Tasha's death will hit the news, particularly after the media attention we've had over the past week or so. And then what? They'll just plonk Ellie back down on the drive and that will be that? It sounds doubtful, but it's all I've got to hope for.

Eventually, after what seems like an interminable amount of time, the phone rings. I dash to answer it before stopping myself. I look at the clock. It's 9.30 p.m. Who answers the phone on its first ring at 9.30 p.m.? I give it a few seconds before picking up.

'Hello?'

'Nick? It's Emma.'

'Oh, hi,' I reply, trying to sound relaxed. 'What's up?'

'I was just wondering if Tasha's left yours yet,' she says, the worry now clear in her voice. 'Only she was meant to be here over an hour ago and I can't get hold of her on her mobile.'

'Really? She left here not long after eight,' I say.

'Shit. Do you think she's alright? Was she going anywhere in between?'

'I dunno,' I say, trying to sound reassuring. 'I'm sure it's fine. I'll try and call her and then ring you back.'

I wait a second before calling Tasha's phone. I know I need to phone her, because it's one of the areas in which people often fall flat on their faces. It's a bit of a giveaway when a husband doesn't even bother to call his wife's phone when he realises she's missing.

The phone goes through to voicemail.

I call Emma back. As I wait for the sound of the ringing to start, all I can think about is not wanting to be the one to find Tasha's body. The phone barely rings once before Emma answers.

'Voicemail,' I say. 'Listen, she walks through Jubilee Park to get to yours. She probably sat down to clear her mind in the fresh air and hasn't realised the time. I'm sure it's fine. You walk over here and I'll walk to yours. We should meet halfway. She can't be far. Might be a good idea to bring Cristina or Leanne with you. One of you needs to stay at yours, though, in case she turns up there.'

'They couldn't make it,' Emma says. 'They had to cancel. It was just going to be me and Tash.'

'Well, I'll leave now and we'll meet halfway,' I reply. 'Keep your phone on you.'

I give it a few minutes, knowing full well that Emma will leave immediately. If I wait a bit, she'll cover more of the journey than I will and is more likely to come across Tasha's body, meaning I won't need to. I'm not sure I can handle it.

After what seems like an age, but the clock on my phone tells me was barely four minutes, I put on my shoes and leave.

I walk purposefully, but not quickly. I don't know how well they can trace the route a person takes using mobile phone tracking, but I don't want this to look anything other than completely natural.

Within a few minutes, I'm at the park. My heart is thudding against my ribcage as I realise what's about to happen. I'm about to find my wife's dead body.

Before I see anything, I hear a voice.

'Nick!' she yells. 'Over here!'

I turn in the direction of the voice and see Emma. One side of her face is lit up by the blue light of her mobile phone, which is pressed up against her ear. She's looking down at the ground, on which all I can see is a dark heap. I know immediately what it is.

I jog over, my whole world slowing down around me as I struggle to process what's going on, even though I've expected it – planned it.

'Yeah, she is,' Emma says into the phone, the panic clear in her voice and on her face. 'Her husband's just arrived.' She swings the phone upwards to move the microphone away from her mouth. 'She's been attacked, Nick.'

I struggle to catch my breath. *Attacked.*

I try to speak. 'Is she . . . is she . . .'

'She's okay,' Emma says. 'She's breathing. The ambulance is on its way.'

All of a sudden, the darkness of Jubilee Park becomes a whole lot darker.

48

NICK

The ambulance goes hell for leather between Jubilee Park and the hospital. *A serious head wound* was what the paramedic said, and it needed treating quickly. *A huge loss of blood.* I toy with the idea of asking them to slow down, but I don't.

She looks almost unrecognisable. The swelling has already started. The paramedics seem to be worried about swelling developing on her brain, so they've booked her in for emergency scans. Seeing your wife covered in blood and knowing that you are responsible for it is one of the hardest things in the world to see. But it's the sickening gurgling noise she makes the whole way there which gets me the most.

When we arrive at the hospital, the paramedics usher me out of the ambulance and a nurse takes me through into the waiting area as the paramedics wheel Tasha out on the stretcher. They disappear through a different set of doors as the nurse tries to reassure me everything will be alright and that Tasha's in safe hands. I have no way of telling her that's not what I want to hear.

I'm given a paper cup of hot, sweet tea – too sweet – and told that a doctor will come to see me shortly to let me know what's going on and to let me see my wife. Emma decides she'd rather have coffee and sets off in search of a machine.

It's all a blur. I've no idea how much time passes. It seems to fly by, yet at the same time it feels interminable. Before long, though, I recognise the familiar voice of McKenna. She's starting to follow me around like a bad fart. I wonder how the hell she found out about this so quickly. Had they been watching? No. That wouldn't be reasonable. I tell myself that the doctors or paramedics probably recognised Tasha or knew who she was from all the recent press attention. They'd know her name. There might even be some sort of marker on the medical records which alerted the police. I don't know, and right now I don't care. All I know is I'm in no state to want to speak to McKenna.

'How is she?' the DI asks as Emma rounds the corner with her paper cup of coffee.

'I don't know,' I say vaguely, surprised at how hoarse and distant my voice sounds.

'Do they know what happened exactly?' she says, looking alternately at both me and Emma.

'Isn't that your job?' I reply, trying to add a biting venom into my tone and quickly realising it's coming naturally.

'We can't speak to her until the doctors have seen her, Nick. I was referring more to what she was doing in the park at this time of night in the first place. Why walk that way? Hardly seems safe. Why didn't she drive? Take a taxi? Get you to give her a lift?'

McKenna's eyes don't leave mine.

'The doctors say it looks as if she was targeted specifically,' she tells me, her voice neutral. 'She had no purse, bag or phone on her so we can only presume the attacker took them from her.'

'A mugging?' I ask.

'That's what it looks like,' she replies, again looking as though she's sussing me out. 'Have you been at home all evening?'

'Yeah,' I reply. 'I only left when Emma called and said Tasha hadn't turned up.'

'On your own, I presume?'

I shrug and force an odd sort of smile, as if to say *Well yeah, unfortunately.* I know I'm on shaky ground with what I'm about to say. I didn't have the opportunity to set up the whole Derek-alibi plan. What with everything else going on, it slipped through my fingers. But after ransacking the man's house and seeing the scared look on his face, I wonder if things might be different this time. After all, it's the only option I have left. The last throw of the dice. I decide it's worth the risk. 'Actually, if you mean can I prove I was at home, yeah, I can. I went out to the front garden a few minutes after Tasha left. Derek was on his drive, putting out his bins.'

'You want to use Derek as your alibi again?' McKenna asks. 'Is that wise?'

'Wait. Alibi?' I say, trying to sound shocked and angry. 'You mean you think I did this?'

'Not at all. What makes you think that? I just need to find out who was where and when. Establish the facts. Tell me about Derek.'

'He was there,' I say. 'He's the only person who saw me. Then I went back inside and nothing else happened until Emma called.'

McKenna nods again. I can see she knows it's unlikely I'd have left home and gone to the park to beat my wife up, especially with the media attention we've had and everyone in the local area knowing our faces. But she knows something's not quite right, I can tell. She just doesn't know what.

We sit in a stony silence for hours, only occasionally punctuated by one of us going to get another cup of tea or coffee or making the usual remarks about hoping we'll hear something soon. We're given updates every hour or so. They're increasingly positive, telling us they've stopped the bleeding, kept it away from her brain and that she's conscious again. What really fucks me off is that McKenna goes to see Tasha twice in the early hours, the doctors seeming to give preference to the police over her own husband.

Around six in the morning, the doctor appears in the doorway and tells us Tasha is stable, but has a bad concussion. She's also lost a lot of blood. 'She'll be weak,' he says.

'Can I see her?' I ask, more to McKenna than the doctor.

'Fine with me,' she says, turning to make eye contact with the doctor, who nods.

I'm led into the ward by McKenna, who smiles as we reach Tasha's bed. She's lying back, her head angled towards the window. It's starting to look like a bright and sunny day out there. It's the first time I've noticed the weather since Ellie disappeared.

'Hi,' I say gently. After a couple of seconds, Tasha moves her head towards me. It's almost zombie-like, and I swear I can hear her neck creaking as she moves.

'Nick,' she whispers, in a deep rasp.

I look at McKenna. That's a good sign, surely? I realise I've found myself pleased that she's alive and recognises me. This shouldn't be the case. I should be gutted. Gutted that she survived the attack. Gutted that Ellie isn't coming back. This whole situation is one enormous mess.

'How are you?' I ask, sitting down on the edge of the bed and tucking a stray lock of hair behind her ear.

'I've been better,' she replies.

'Did you see who did this to you?'

She shakes her head slowly. 'It was dark. He came from behind. I don't remember anything.'

'The doctor reckons there's no permanent damage,' McKenna says. 'Her cheekbone is fractured and she'll have a lot of bruising for a while, which'll hurt. But she's a tough little cookie, your wife. She's a fighter.'

'She certainly is,' I say, looking at Tasha. 'She certainly is.'

49

NICK

Once we're both back from the hospital, I take some time to get Tasha upstairs to bed. She was adamant she didn't want to stay in hospital, and even the doctors could see there was no point arguing with her. Even after something like that, she's still headstrong and knows exactly what she wants. And she knows she's going to get it, too, because she'll always make sure of it.

She might know what she wants, but she doesn't always know what she needs. That's Tasha's problem. She's going to need to rest for a few days, at the very least. Not only will it help her to recuperate, but it should give me some breathing space as well.

I can't help but have massively conflicted emotions. I'm both relieved that the attack didn't work and angry at the person who did it. Even though I knew it was coming, even though I arranged it, my last-minute change of heart makes me furious at Geoff for having gone through with it after I'd asked him not to. And then to see my wife lying there in that state in the hospital. It's not something I'd wish on my worst enemy. Knowing that it was all my fault made it a hundred times worse. The guilt was unbearable.

My first instinct is to get round to Alan's house and fire off a dark web message to Geoff, but I don't have the faintest idea what I'd say. I want to rip the guy's throat out, but I know I need to remain calm and collected. I'm pleased, in a way, that I'm a different guy to the one all those years back. I'm glad that I'm a little calmer, a little less likely to snap and make a fool of myself. I'm able to think things through a little more, stop myself from going round there and kicking his fucking head in.

I take a deep breath and close my eyes. It's time to think straight. The deeper I get in, the more I need to focus and think about what I'm doing. It's not too late. It's never too late. Back downstairs, I make myself a cup of coffee and sit quietly at the kitchen table. I need to keep some semblance of normality. Something to anchor myself in everyday life and retain some focus.

I can't go getting the police involved in this. I need to avoid that at all costs. How do you tell the local detectives that you organised for your wife to be murdered, but it's alright because she only got beaten up? I can't tell them anything about what's happened. If I tell them about Jen Hood's emails now, they'll want to know why they weren't told earlier. I'm in far too deep, and there's nothing I can do but try to get myself out of it without digging myself in any further.

The evidence that I had, the evidence that I could have taken to the police at the start, is now gone. It's unusable. They're going to take one look at those emails, link them to the fact that Tasha was the victim of a random violent attack a few days later and start to put two and two together. Why didn't I just go to them at the start and let them know what had happened? Why didn't I just show them the email? I know why – because I'm a stubborn bastard who thought he could work his own way out of it. Super Nick to the rescue again. But this time I failed. Big time.

Now I need to find Ellie myself, but where do I start? I'm completely on my own with this one.

The obvious thing to do would be to ask questions. But then I don't think I'm exactly going to get Jen Hood's life story or a scan of their driving licence back by return of email. If this person wanted me to know who they were, they would have given me more details by now.

I try to think if there might be some more abstract, out-of-the-box ways to get the information I need. Lateral thinking, they call it. Perhaps lay a few trails, a couple of red herrings. Slip in some false information about me and Tasha and see if they pick up on it.

I try to think back to some of the research I've done into personality disorders and the effects they can have on people. Would the kidnapper be a psychopath or a sociopath? Who would want to kidnap a child and demand the mother be killed in return? All I know is that it's not the sort of person I want to be messing about with.

50

NICK

Having switched on my laptop and opened my web browser, I fight the urge to download Tor and log on to the dark web. A large part of me desperately wants to see if Geoff has been in touch – see what he has to say for himself – but I can't risk it. That connection now has to be completely severed. Instead, I check my emails.

I don't know how so many people have found my email address, but there's a deluge of messages from complete strangers giving me their theories as to what happened to Ellie. Perhaps predictably, a number of them accuse me, Tasha or both of us of killing her and hiding her body. Some of the messages contain the most vile abuse I've ever read, but right now that's washing over me. I know they're wrong, and soon enough so will they.

Some of the friendlier theories are actually even wackier. A couple are convinced they have evidence of alien spacecraft being in the area on the day Ellie disappeared, some are certain they know where she is through dowsing and looking at ley lines, others that they've seen visions in their dreams that reveal Ellie's location.

I scroll through, reading a few lines of each email, becoming increasingly worried about the mental state of some people in the world. One, though, catches my eye. I read it again more closely.

> *You should look at Lynda Macauley. I hope you find your daughter.*

Below it is an address in Halifax, West Yorkshire. Another crank who wants to frame his neighbour. Great. I fire off what has become my stock response to people who've got a suspicion which doesn't involve aliens or ghosts.

> *If you have some information which may help, please call Detective Inspector Jane McKenna.*

As I hit the 'Send' button, the doorbell goes. I look out the front window and see McKenna stood at the door. Nice timing. I head into the hallway and open the door, standing aside to let her through.

'How's Tasha?' she asks.

'Yeah, she's okay. Just tired and shaken, I think.' *I'm fine, too, thanks for asking.*

'Probably best she rests. Takes it out of you, something like that,' she says as she sits down in the living room. 'You'll need to keep a close eye on her. Quite often it's the mental scarring that does the most damage. Can really knock someone's confidence, something like that. Once she's feeling better physically, it's best to get her out the house again. Get back on the horse as quickly as possible.'

'That's the plan,' I say. 'Funny, isn't it? How Tasha and I have spent most of our lives living in complete normality, wanting to escape and do something different, and now we're spending every waking minute trying to regain normality again.' McKenna just smiles. 'I can't describe how bizarre it feels to be living this sort of nightmare. Unable to live a normal life in your own home.'

'Being invaded every day by police officers,' she adds, smiling.

'Yeah, that too.' I smile as well. It feels weird.

'Which reminds me,' she says. 'It was Derek who you say saw you last night, wasn't it?'

'Yeah,' I reply. 'Why? Don't tell me he's denied that, too.'

McKenna smiles. 'No, he didn't deny it. He said he saw you. He actually went into great detail about how he saw you rush out of the house after Tasha and skidded to a halt when you saw him watching, and that you then slunk back inside. Why did you do that, Nick?'

I swallow. 'Do what?' I ask, not even thinking about what I'm saying.

'Why did you race after her?'

'Uh, she forgot something,' I say.

'What did she forget?'

'Hmm?'

'What did she forget, Nick?'

My brain's racing at a thousand miles an hour, but going nowhere useful. 'Her phone,' I say.

'Her phone? Is that why Emma couldn't reach her when she called to find out where she was?'

I feel suddenly relieved. 'Yeah. Probably.'

'So why didn't you hear the phone ringing when Emma called? In fact, why did you try to call Tasha's phone to find out where she was after Emma called you to say she hadn't turned up? Surely if you knew she had left her phone at home, you wouldn't have tried calling her.'

'I forgot. Force of habit,' I say, my insides feeling like they're on fire.

McKenna nods. 'Right. So the phone's in the house somewhere is it?'

I shake my head. 'I dunno. I presume so. Does it matter?'

'Possibly not,' she replies. 'Mind if I have a look for it?'

'Yeah, I do actually,' I say. McKenna stops dead in her tracks. 'Tasha's only just got out of hospital. I'd really rather you didn't go around ransacking the house right now. It's a phone. It can wait.'

McKenna looks at me, a stern look in her eyes. 'That phone could prove to be important evidence in a case of violent assault on your wife, Nick.'

'No, it couldn't. Because she didn't take it with her to the park, did she? It was here the whole time, so it's not evidence at all.'

'Unless you're somehow mistaken and she did take it with her.'

'In which case there's no point searching the house, is there?' I think that's what they call having the upper hand. McKenna knows it, too, and changes tack.

'Don't you want us to catch the person who did this to Tasha?'

'Of course I do,' I reply.

'Why did you stop when you saw Derek and then go back inside the house? Surely you wouldn't want Tasha walking through the park without her phone, would you?' Before I can answer, she's fired another question at me. 'Your back door leads through your garden to a footpath, doesn't it? You can reach Jubilee Park from there. I suppose you could've taken that route to give Tasha her phone back, couldn't you?'

She's bombarding me with questions. I know exactly what she's doing, but I can't stop it and I can't deal with it. Tasha never used that footpath. She hated it. But I can't find the words to say that.

'Well, I—'

'Which begs the question as to why you didn't just keep on up the road; why you stopped as soon as you saw Derek. Did you take a route to Jubilee Park which'd make you less likely to be seen?'

'Can I get a glass of water?' I ask. 'I'm feeling really weird.'

I keep my face relatively neutral, but inside I'm screaming.

51

TASHA

The doctors at the hospital didn't seem to get it. Every time they asked me how I felt, I told them I felt nothing. No, my head didn't hurt. No, my joints weren't stiff. Compared to what I've been going through over the past few days, any physical pain is completely irrelevant. Bring it on, I say.

I have no idea what happened. All I remember is hearing that single footstep. That's the weirdest thing. It wasn't like someone was walking towards me or jumping out from somewhere. Just one footstep. As if they were stood waiting, just inside the shadows, waiting for someone to come past. Waiting for me to come past.

The police asked me in the hospital if I'd had anything with me at the time of the attack. I told them I couldn't remember, but that I didn't usually leave the house empty-handed. I couldn't remember if I had any money on me. Probably not. I don't think I would have taken a handbag because I was only going over to a friend's house and wouldn't have needed any money. Besides which, a woman walking around on her own at night with a handbag becomes a target. They asked me about my phone, but I don't know. I think I must have taken it with me. It's not here now, but I don't care about that. I don't want to phone anyone. I don't want anyone phoning me. I just want to curl up and die.

Jane McKenna is downstairs now, but I don't want to see her. I can hear Nick and her talking, but I can't work out what they're saying. I don't want to, either, unless she's come to say that they've found Ellie.

I know I'm wallowing, and I hate it. It isn't me. I'm the sort of person who picks myself back up and gets on with things, but it really isn't that easy right now. I've turned the bedroom TV off because it's full of mind-numbing crap. Don't get me wrong, my mind definitely needs numbing, but that sort of trash just isn't distracting enough. I can still hear my thoughts, dark and intrusive. I don't want to hear them. I want them gone. I need to be able to concentrate on something for just long enough to allow the fog to lift, to not feel as though the whole world has imploded on me. I need a sense of normality.

I groan as I lean over and pick up my laptop bag from beside the bed, my ribs and arm telling me they're not keen. I landed awkwardly, according to the doctors. I'm not quite sure how I could have landed any less awkwardly; I'm pretty sure I was unconscious before I hit the ground. Either way, my body's paying for it now.

I unzip the laptop bag and pull the silver machine out, opening it up and switching it on. The welcome noise is reassuring, solid. It's recognisable. I used to hear it every day, back when things were normal. Back when I had my daughter. Back when everything was just as it should have been. Before my life got turned upside down.

There are one hundred and nine emails in my work inbox. I scroll down the list and see a few that I can imagine are from colleagues offering their best wishes and sympathies on hearing about Ellie going missing. I don't want to read those, so I stick with opening ones that have blatantly work-related subject lines. Most are just things that I've been copied into by my team or by people who like to copy forty names into an email that only needs to be seen by one. Right now, though, I'm grateful for those people. It means I can sit and read what's been going on, forcing my brain to concentrate on something else without needing to do any actual work. I feel involved. I feel wanted again.

I actually find work incredibly relaxing. So many people find it stressful and need to find ways to relax after work. For me, it's the other way round. I find it very calming, almost therapeutic. It requires just the right level of brainpower and just the right level of routine. It's a bit like knitting or painting – you need to be focused, but you also know what you're doing the whole time. It's a perfect balance.

Do I feel guilty for opening up my laptop and reading work emails while the police are out searching high and low for my missing daughter? Yes, perhaps a bit, but it does what it needs to do. Some people turn to drink or drugs, I turn to work. I don't think anyone would begrudge me hitting the bottle in this situation, so the only difference is that my laptop isn't going to damage my liver.

Strangely, I can feel my headache starting to dissipate as I read through the emails. One is a thread of twenty-six messages talking about a discrepancy on some accounts. Nothing that even concerns or interests me, but reading through it and having been included on the message makes me feel important again. It sounds strange to say, but it's true. And just for a few fleeting moments, I'm able to forget everything and pretend – just briefly – that everything is back to the way it was.

52

NICK

McKenna's gone. She told me – eventually, after watching me squirm – that the CCTV at the end of the footpath, next to the corner shop, shows that I didn't get that far. She knows I didn't go to Jubilee Park last night. Somehow, that makes it even worse. She could see that something wasn't right and she pressed and pressed, watching me wriggle as I tried to answer her questions, knowing the answers to them anyway. I'm pretty sure that's got to be illegal. There's a reason why she keeps turning up on her own, asking these probing questions and more or less accusing me of things.

That's because she knows something isn't quite right. I think she knows I didn't attack Tasha. But she's not stupid. She spends her life talking to people who are trying to hide something from her. She knows I'm hiding something and she's determined to find out what it is. That's why she was putting the pressure on, trying to trip me up. All she knows at the moment is what *didn't* happen.

I'm still shaking. I've downed three pints of water, trying to stop my head from spinning round in circles. I can feel the net closing in on me, and I don't like it one bit. I'm not going to lie – I'm beginning to panic. I'm starting to get desperate. I need to think clearly. What can she know, where can she be digging and what can she find? I need to start thinking like the police, thinking logically and trying to work out where I can go next.

Despite Derek's alibi and the CCTV footage showing that I can't have done it myself, I'm starting to panic that McKenna might trace Tasha's attack back to me. What if they find the person who did it? What if he caves in and confesses? What if he comes to some sort of plea bargain with the police and McKenna comes knocking?

They can't prove a thing. I know they can't. Okay, so I spoke to Mark. I met up with an old school friend. What of it? And yeah, I was in the Talbot Arms and I spoke to Warren. That doesn't mean a thing. There's no way they can link the attack to Warren. At that point they'll probably work out what went on, but they can't prove a thing.

All of these thoughts whizz around my head, barely registering before they disappear again and make way for another.

I go to pour myself another glass of water but opt for something stronger.

After a second glass of whisky, I decide to head upstairs. When I get there, Tasha's sitting up in bed with the laptop on her knees, replying to an email.

'What are you doing?' I ask.

'Working.'

'Come on, Tash,' I say, trying to keep the anger out of my voice. 'I think you can take a few days off work seeing as you've just been mugged and your daughter has gone missing. They might just give you that much.'

'I can't afford the time off,' she replies, not even bothering to take her eyes off the screen.

'They can't begrudge you the time off. You've got a legal right to it,' I tell her.

'It's not like that. That's not how it works. I've already missed important meetings.'

'So what? They can have someone else do your work while you're away,' I say, trying to convince her.

Finally, she looks at me. There's anger in her eyes.

'Do you have any idea the sacrifices I've made for my career?' she says. I feel like telling her yes, she's sacrificed everything for it, including a decent family life and a moral compass. 'I've worked so hard to get as far as I have, and now it's all going to go to waste because I'm stuck here at home and other people are picking up my work and my clients. Is that really what you want?'

I snap. 'How the hell can you only be thinking about work when your daughter is missing? What's wrong with you?' She sits and stares blankly at me so I let loose, giving her both barrels. 'You've never cared about Ellie, have you? Or me. It's always been your career. Your perfect image. Your own needs. You leave me at home to look after *our* daughter while you go off following your career.'

'Nick, just because I've got a proper job and you haven't, I don't think—'

I don't hear any more as I slam the bedroom door and head back downstairs for another night on the sofa.

53

NICK

This sofa's starting to feel more familiar than my own bed. That can only be a bad sign, but it's a hell of a lot better than sleeping upstairs with the dragon.

I've switched off push notifications for email on my phone. Every time the thing buzzed it nearly gave me a heart attack. Of course, it was always spam or a newsletter from a company I once bought a pen from eight years ago.

I need to regain some control, so now I only check my emails manually. I'm being extra cautious, but by now I'm pretty sure my emails aren't being monitored. Plus, it's probably illegal. I'm not naïve enough to think that these things don't go on, but I've got to draw the line somewhere or the paranoia will finish me.

I open the Mail app on my phone and five messages ping through. That's just from the last couple of hours. Funnily enough, the concerned messages from family and friends seem to have stopped and there are just four newsletters and another email from Jen Hood.

To keep myself calm and focused, I methodically delete each of the other four emails first. I've got to keep a level head. Then, fingers shaking, I open Jen Hood's email. The subject line is *Ellie* and the email has just the words *The password is Natasha*, followed by a Vimeo link.

I click the link and it takes me straight to a Vimeo page. The text on the screen says *This is a password-protected video. Do you have the password to watch this private video?* It sounds weird, but I'm really fucked off by the picture of a hand being held palm out like some sort of jumped-up nightclub bouncer. I try to remain calm and type Natasha's name in the password field. I hit 'Submit'.

The next page loads everything instantly except the video itself, which seems to be taking an age, hidden behind a plain white box. I'm on the verge of throwing the phone out of the window, but then my screen changes and the video loads. It's now a black box. I press the 'Play' button and turn my phone sideways to get the full-screen view.

After a couple of seconds, the black screen fades to a blurred shot of what could be any young girl. It's the whimpering I recognise first, which is bizarre, because it's not a whimpering I've heard before. It certainly isn't the usual whimpering, like on that morning when she forgot the picture of Miss Williams. It's pained, desperate, real.

'Daddy, I want to come home,' she says as the picture begins to clear and the tears start to cloud my eyes. 'Please can you do what you have to do so I can come home.' She begins to cry. They say love's just a chemical reaction in the brain, but I can feel the pain in my chest as I hear her pained desperation. Just as quickly as it started, the video ends.

I'm lost, completely lost. One part of me wants to watch it over and over again, but another part knows I can't bear to. I close the Vimeo page and my email inbox reappears, this time with another new email. It doesn't even register at first – I'm still in pieces – but before long I realise it's another email from Jen Hood. I open it and read the text.

> *I'm glad to see you've finally seen what it is you have to do, but it's just not good enough. I want her dead, not just injured. You'll need to try harder. She has to die or you will never see Ellie again. Don't even bother trying to track us down. I can see everything you're doing. One false move and you will never see her again. You know what to do.*

My hands shaking, I close the email app and lock my phone. I need another drink.

54

NICK

I'm in a quandary. My initial instinct is to take the video to the police. After all, they'll be able to trace it, won't they? All of this talk of killing Tasha to free Ellie seems completely irrelevant when I can see my baby girl crying on a video screen, begging to come home. This needs to end now.

But if I show the police, the first thing they'll want to know is why I didn't tell them earlier about Jen Hood's emails. What possible reason have I got for not wanting to tell the police that a stranger offered me the chance to get my daughter back by killing my wife? Apart from the obvious, that is.

Besides which, it'd completely remove that option for me. The only avenue it would leave is putting my complete faith in the police to find whoever's taken Ellie and save her before it's too late. I quickly realise that's a level of faith I just don't have. I need to keep my options open, and coming clean to the police about the Jen Hood thing would take those options away from me, not to mention leaving me under a huge amount of suspicion.

I wonder if I could get away with showing them the video but not the emails. Problem is, they'd want to know where the video came from. They'd have their forensics people all over it and just deleting the other emails wouldn't be enough to get past them. And how suspicious would that look?

I think about putting the video on a memory stick and claiming it was pushed through my door or sent in the post or something. Would they be able to tell? I don't understand enough about computers to know if they'd be able to see that the video originally came from an email. Can they track things like that? I could look online and research it to find out, but what if they discovered that, too?

I'm quickly coming to realise that every tiny potential move could have huge ramifications. Even the quickest Google search could unravel the whole thing. Funny thing is, I've not even done anything illegal. I haven't kidnapped Ellie. I haven't threatened to murder a child. I've done nothing wrong. All I did was leave her in the car for a minute. Two, tops. Does that really warrant this level of paranoia? Yeah, at a push the attack on Tasha could be considered my fault, but hell, I didn't actually do it myself.

What's wrong with me? I'm now trying to justify organising a hit on my wife. The worst fucking hit of all time, too, it seems. What if Tasha saw her attacker? What if she identifies him later? What if the guy is caught and crumbles and the whole thing leads back to me? He's obviously not the most calm and collected bloke in the world if he couldn't finish the job properly.

All of these thoughts fly through my head at once. I can hear them screaming as they rattle around inside my skull, all vying for attention as I struggle to keep it together. That's how most first-time killers are caught, they say. Their brain just can't comprehend what's happened or keep up with all of the different thoughts and emotions. The whole 'carry on as normal' thing just doesn't happen.

I've seen countless parents of missing or murdered children on TV over the years, all talking about how their world stopped turning the day their child disappeared from their life. It certainly becomes a different sort of world. A world of different colours, of different moods. It's as if all of the colour has just fallen out of the world, drained away to somewhere else; a parallel world where everything carried on as normal, where nothing ever happened. But, weirdly, that parallel world is still there, still visible. It's the one that everyone around me is still living in. They still see the colour. Their world is still turning.

For me, the world stopped turning that morning Ellie disappeared. And I'm the only one who can start it moving again.

55

NICK

The bottle of scotch is looking desperately empty, but I'm starting to feel a whole lot better. I'm starting to think clearly for the first time in days, and I've got the bottle to thank for that.

It's been a long time since I drank this amount. I've always been afraid, scared that I might turn into the sort of monster I turned into that night with Angela. Now, though, I don't feel like I'm turning into a monster at all. In fact, I'm thinking far more clearly, far more lucidly. I'm not stupid enough to think that the thoughts I'm having now are the ones I'd have sober, but at least I'm thinking them clearly. Whatever I do, I've got to do something. Sitting around and doing nothing isn't an option. Not since getting that video of Ellie.

So I've had to make a decision. It's not now about simply getting Ellie back. It's about saving her life. The kidnapper has already told me he'll kill Ellie if I don't do what he wants me to do, and I can't take that risk. I'm well aware that in my current mental state killing Tasha means I'll likely be caught. That's a risk I'm willing to take. I'd rather spend a lifetime in prison and know that Ellie is safe than have a life of freedom should something happen to her. What sort of freedom would that be? That would be the worst sort of prison, one from which there would be no hope of ever escaping.

Again, I run through the ideas I've had as to how I can do it. It's going to take some forethought and planning, but I also need to do it quickly. There was definite malice in that email, and I really believe that whoever's got Ellie intends to do exactly as they said. I want – *need* – Ellie safe, and I need her safe now.

I stand to go upstairs and get my laptop, but stop myself. I want to look up ways of doing it. I'm no longer worried about the police monitoring the laptop and seeing what I'm looking at. Ellie is what matters. The only reason I don't want to go into the bedroom is because I know I'll end up doing it there and then, and that won't end well for anybody.

I just want to escape this madness. I'm starting to think that I really might not ever see Ellie again. If that's the case, there's no point carrying on. If I can't bring myself to do what needs doing, I might as well just end it all now. The end result will be the same, but much quicker and far less painful.

Tasha's been taking Tramadol to help with the pain since the attack. I wonder how many of those I'd need to finish myself off. Or I could finish her off. I could crush a few up and put them in her food to get that job done, but McKenna would spot that a mile off. No, I can't do that. I've got to do myself in. And it sounds weird, but I wouldn't want to kill myself with Tasha's painkillers. Not the ones she's on because of me. No, her sleeping tablets would work far better. Far less guilt involved there. Could've just been accidental, right? I think about how many temazepam I'd need to sleep forever. Maybe I should google it. Probably not a great idea; I imagine they'd have cars swooping down the road in seconds, dragging me away before I'd even got the packet open.

I can feel myself beginning to crash, but I need to stay awake. I'm not thinking straight, but at least I'm thinking.

I go back to my inbox and open the last email from Jen Hood again. I figure that if I desensitise myself to it, I'll be able to think more clearly. I need to get past the reactionary stuff and start to look at the situation with a fresh mind. I swallow hard as I click the link for the video again.

Ellie's voice catches my heart, and I realise I'm going to have to watch this a fair few times if I'm even going to come close to being desensitised to it. I'm soon no longer aware of any sound, though, as my eyes are drawn to something over Ellie's left shoulder, half hanging out of a cardboard box. I pause the video.

I can't quite make out what it is, but it looks very familiar. I squint at the screen, my nose barely inches away from it. Then I realise.

It's a jumper. One I've seen before. Many times. In fact, I've seen it on many people. But in this instant, I know exactly whose that jumper is.

56

The smoke fills the room with a steady haze as the music fills our ears. It's a pure sensory experience: the sweet smell of the smoke, the softness of the bed under our legs, the warmth of her body pressed against mine. Even the yellowy gold of the university logo seems to gleam brightly on the breast of the jumper that's slung over the chair at the end of the bed. I'm starting to tune most of it out, though. I've got other things on my mind.

They say your university days are the best of your life. Mine have been pretty good to me, and I didn't even go to uni. I still got to enjoy all the best bits, though. The drinks, the parties, the girls. One of the joys of having friends studying locally. All the fun without any of the hassle. Deadlines and debt. An eternal life of learning. Nope, not for me.

She rests her head on my shoulder, her long hair flowing down my chest. I know I've got to tell her sometime – I've been meaning to for a while – but she's not the sort of girl who can be let down gently. I don't know that for sure as I've never dared to try, but a few things have made me wonder whether she might not react in the best way to what I have to tell her.

She's a quiet sort, never one to seem as though she'd blow up in your face, but they always say it's the quiet ones you have to watch out for. I never really knew what that meant until I met her. Until then, quiet girls had always been just that: quiet. But with her it seems as though there's something else bubbling away under the surface. It's not something I can really put my finger on, but it's there. I know it is.

I decide I need to cut to the chase. Regardless of anything else, it's not fair on me or her to carry on as if there's nothing wrong. I need to tell her, and I need to tell her now before it gets any worse for both of us.

'What are you thinking?' she asks, as if she can read my mind. That's exactly the sort of thing that makes me wonder about her. Nothing I can explain, but weird and kind of creepy at the same time. As if she already knows.

'Not much,' I say, immediately chiding myself for chickening out. 'Just stuff.'

'What sort of stuff?' she asks.

'Life. Just stuff in general.' I don't know why I can't just come out with it. All of a sudden the words seem to have left me. It's not a problem I've ever had before – I usually have far too much to say – but this time she seems to have caught me on the back foot.

'Us?' she asks, stroking my chest. As quiet and meek as she seems, I can tell that she really gets off on being coquettish when she wants to be.

'Yeah, I guess so,' I reply, pausing as I think of what to say. 'I just wonder whether this is something that can carry on.'

I feel her stiffen slightly before she speaks, but she doesn't lift her head from my shoulder. She just lies there, not moving, as if she's trying to process the thought over and over again. I can tell that I've upset her.

'How do you mean?' she says, calmly and innocently.

'Well, I mean, you'll be finished here in a few weeks. Back off home, probably, or away on new adventures, finding a job.'

She speaks without emotion. 'But you live here, Nick. You're not going anywhere. You said as much yourself. And I love the place. I don't want to go anywhere. I want to find a job here and stay. We could even find jobs together.'

This is what I was worried about. 'I dunno. I just wonder if it'd be the same after uni. Life's different once you get out into the real world. I wouldn't want that to spoil what we've got. I know so many people who've said that.'

'Like who?' she asks, this time accusingly.

'Just friends,' I say.

There's a deathly silence for a good minute or so, neither of us speaking. I can almost tell what she's thinking, following her thought processes in my head as she lies there breathing, more deeply with every breath.

Eventually, she speaks.

'It's not that at all, is it? You've met someone else.' There's pain and anguish in her voice. I knew I should have said all this earlier before she got too attached. And now I'm going to have to deal with a psychotic bunny boiler for the next few weeks.

'Don't be daft,' I say, trying to defuse the situation.

'No, it's true, isn't it? Who is it? Really, I won't mind.' Her voice has changed completely. Now she sounds calm again, confident almost.

I know for a fact she will mind, though. There's no way on earth I can tell her. If she knew, it would kill her. 'I haven't met anyone,' I tell her.

'Is it Tash?'

I force a laugh and shake my head. 'No, Emma. It's not Tash. I promise.'

57

NICK

It was the jumper that did it. The old university jumper that so many people at the uni had. I remember the first day I spoke to Emma and noticed that the badge on hers was slightly different.

The university had a rather bizarre emblem that was emblazoned across everything: a pelican with a pen in its mouth. It was some obscure reference to a half-famous writer who once went to the university years ago. Only Emma had altered hers by undoing the stitching on the embroidered badge and replacing the pen with an embroidered spliff. It was a very bold but understated move from someone so quiet and reserved. Almost like a silent protest. Most people didn't notice, and if they had she probably would've got into a lot of trouble, but it was one of the things that first attracted me to her.

I think back to that day in her dorm room, when I told her I was ending our relationship. Now it all makes sense. She'd reacted so calmly that day, it could only ever have meant one thing. They say it's the calm ones you need to watch out for. The ones who bottle it all up, planning ahead, quietly working away in the background while everyone worries about the hotheads who are blowing their lids.

I'd been right back then when I suspected Emma would react badly. I could tell as we were speaking that she was devastated but didn't want to say anything. I think I wanted to believe she was just holding it all in, trying to put a brave face on things. But now I see it for what it really was.

I can also see why Emma was right back on the scene, acting like the caring and concerned friend. She needed to know the inside scoop. Needed to make sure I didn't mention the Jen Hood emails to anyone. Wanted to know what the police were doing and when. Like the criminal returning to the scene of the crime to witness the fallout. Realising this now makes me feel physically sick.

Did she know that I'd asked her to invite Tasha over because that's when the attack was planned? No. She couldn't have done. It's impossible. But my heart lurches as I remember something else: Emma said that Cristina and Leanne had cancelled that night so it was just going to be the two of them. Just Emma and Tasha. Why was that? Was she going to take the opportunity to kill her herself? If so, why didn't she just do that weeks, months, years ago? If she wanted Tasha dead, why not kill her? She probably knew she wouldn't get away with it. Couldn't bring herself to do it. Maybe recently she'd felt the net closing in and realised it might be the only way. It still doesn't explain it properly, but right now my brain is a huge muddle.

It's strange. Some things are becoming far more confusing, but a lot of things are a whole lot clearer. I can't believe I didn't see it earlier. Perhaps I was blind to it. Perhaps I didn't want to think about it. Emma played the long game, and she played it well. All these years she's waited, watching me and Tasha getting together after I told her we weren't an item, watching us get married and try and fail to have kids. What was going through her mind at that point? Was she delighting in watching us crack and fall apart? And what effect did it have on her when we finally conceived and Ellie was born?

I think back, trying to work out at what point I could have spotted things going wrong. Emma had seemed genuinely pleased when Tasha and I finally told her we were going out. The weirdest thing is, that didn't strike me as odd back then. I guess I was too loved up and too involved in the whole situation to even see it. I suppose I just assumed she was actually over it. I couldn't have been more wrong.

The day Ellie was born, Emma was one of the first people to see her. I remember how she just stood staring at her, with what I thought was wonder and amazement in her eyes. Now I know what that look really meant. That was the day her life really changed and she knew there was no going back. She knew she was going to have to do something drastic.

But why now? Why wait until Ellie was five? What significance did that have? Probably none. Perhaps it was just the point at which everything had piled up and she finally snapped. Why that morning? Did she happen to just be passing or coming to see us for some reason and decided on a whim to take her chance? In a way I hope so, because the alternative is that she must have been watching, morning after morning, following us. But I take some comfort in the fact that if that's true then I really can't blame myself. She would've done it sooner or later, whenever the right moment came.

Either way, it's all academic. Right now, my priority is getting Ellie back.

I'm shaking as I put my shoes on and leave the house. I decide to go by foot. I'm not quite sure why, whether I think it'll be easier to lose anyone who's following me – not that it matters, seeing as I'm about to sort this all out once and for all. Besides, I don't fancy having a drink-driving charge added to my list right now. When I get to Jubilee Park, I break from a jog into a sprint.

Eventually, I reach Emma's house. Before I walk up the path, I stop for a moment to compose myself and catch my breath. If Ellie's here, she's probably safe. As soon as Emma is surprised or caught unawares, that could all end. I'm acutely aware that Emma holds all the cards right now.

I ring the doorbell. A few moments later, I hear footsteps, and then Emma opens the door. I give her my best smile and say hello.

58

NICK

'Nick, come in,' she says. 'Is everything okay?'

'Yeah, fine,' I say. 'I went for a walk. Trying to clear my mind, you know. I was passing so thought I'd pop by and say hi.'

'Oh, right. Well, I was just off to bed in a bit. Long day tomorrow. Do you want a drink or something?'

'Just a glass of water would be great,' I say, my throat parched from the run.

'Nothing stronger? You've had a couple already. I can smell it. I thought you'd cut down.'

I smile and let out a small chuckle.

'Rumbled. Go on, then,' I say.

We walk through into her living room. It's paining me to have to go through this charade, knowing that Ellie is probably sitting up in the attic wondering what's happened. Every fibre of my being wants to just take Emma clean out, right here and now, and rush upstairs to grab my daughter. But something inside me stops me.

It's the rational logic that Emma's had years to plan this. She's unlikely to have missed much. It's not as if I'm just going to be able to shimmy up the loft ladder, grab Ellie and go. What if she's booby-trapped it somehow?

There's a good chance the stress, lack of sleep and alcohol are making me think crazy thoughts, but this is hardly a normal situation.

Whichever way I look at it, though, I need to get to the point.

I make sure I've positioned myself closer to the doorway. Closer to the kitchen, too, should a weapon be needed.

'So how are you bearing up?' she asks. She's a good actress. She always was.

'I've had better times,' I reply. 'I was thinking today, actually, about the uni days. How we didn't have any of the stresses of adulthood.'

A nostalgic smile spreads across Emma's face. 'I think about those days a lot,' she says.

'Tash doesn't. I think she just saw it as a means to an end. Most people have their graduation photos on the wall. Tash has just thrown hers in the loft somewhere, along with her jumper and everything.'

'Her jumper?'

'Yeah. Her university one. The one with the logo on.'

Emma's smile has faded slightly. Not much, but it's noticeable. 'Why a jumper of all things?'

'Why not?' I reply. 'Where did you put yours?'

She swallows. 'I don't know. I don't remember. It was a long time ago.'

'It's probably in your loft,' I say, readying myself. 'What else is up there?'

Emma is silent for a few moments.

'Nick, what's this all about?'

I keep my face neutral.

'I've worked it all out. I've been reading the whole situation wrongly for years. You never got over us, did you? You never came to terms with me getting together with Tasha, and when Ellie was born it crushed you. Didn't it?'

Emma's voice is calm and quiet. 'You don't know what you're saying.' She seems almost emotionless now, and that's what scares me the most. Angry, I can deal with. Upset, fine. But this cold, impassive voice and vacant look in her eyes is starting to worry me.

'No, I know exactly what I'm saying,' I tell her. 'And I know exactly where Ellie is.'

'You don't know a thing,' she replies, this time firmer. She seems to have a steely resolve.

All I can do is nod and look at her, my eyes searing into her as I try to calm myself and ensure that I make the right moves to keep Ellie safe. The last thing I want is for Emma to flip and harm her. She could harm me, too. For all I know she could have a knife concealed up her sleeve. She's a lot closer to the side cabinet than I am, too. She could pull anything from one of those drawers before I'd even manage to get close. 'Why Jen Hood?' I ask her.

Emma's head snaps towards me. This has clearly shocked her. But that look only lasts for a brief second before the calm descends again and she smiles. 'It's an anagram, Nick. I would've thought a clever man like you could work out something as basic as that. *John Doe*. The anonymous man. It didn't matter who Jen Hood was. She could've been any old John Doe.'

I shake my head. 'You're insane.'

'That's what you think,' she replies, like a petulant schoolgirl. I feel slightly relieved that my insult didn't rile her. I regretted it as soon as I said it, but now I realise I can get away with pushing a little harder.

'Tell me why, Emma. Tell me why you wanted me to kill Tasha.' I try to say this in a way that's calming, understanding. Deep down, that's what all people want, isn't it?

'Because I loved you, Nick. I still do love you. Do you have any idea what that means?'

'I know what it means to most people,' I say. 'But I'm not quite sure what it means to psychopaths.'

She raises her voice for the first time. 'I am not a psychopath!' She blinks and reverts to her calm quietness. 'Ellie is safe. She's far safer with me than she is with *her*, anyway.'

'I don't doubt that,' I say, meaning every word. 'But she needs to be back with her parents.' Emma says nothing, so I ask her another question that's been burning away at me since I realised it was her. 'Why try to get me to kill Tasha? If you wanted us to be together, why would you risk me getting arrested and thrown in jail? Then you wouldn't have had me anyway. Why not just hire a hitman?'

'Because I wanted you to prove it, Nick. I wanted you to prove your love for me. I should have been her mother,' Emma replies, choked. It's the first sign of any emotion I've seen from her in years.

'How would that prove anything?' I ask. 'That doesn't make any sense.'

'It does,' she replies, as if I'm the mad one. 'She should have been ours.'

I shake my head. 'That doesn't change the fact that she isn't. She's mine. Mine and Tasha's.'

'It would have kept us together, Nick. It would have changed everything. She was the only thing keeping you and Tasha together, too. But you don't have her any more. I do. You need to come back to me.'

I laugh involuntarily. 'I can't do that. She's not our child. She's mine and Tasha's.'

Emma moves towards me far more quickly than I can even anticipate. I go to defend myself, but something stops me. It catches me unawares because her movement is not threatening, not violent; it's smooth and fluid.

She's pressed up against me, trying to kiss me, forcing her tongue into my mouth and her hand down the front of my jeans. I keep my teeth clamped shut and struggle against her, trying to push her away from me.

'Let's do it, Nick,' she says. 'Let's have one of our own. Let's secure our love.'

I wriggle free and push her as hard as I can. It's all I have. It all seems to happen in slow motion. She stumbles backwards and groans like a wounded animal as her head bounces off the corner of the coffee table.

I take my chance and head for the stairs.

59

NICK

I take the stairs two at a time, my feet pounding down on them as I yell Ellie's name. When I get to the top of the stairs, I realise I've never been up here before. I'm disorientated. In all the years Emma's lived here, we've never been invited upstairs. Not that we should have been, but it strikes me as odd.

There was never any reason. We've only been here probably a handful of times, and that was always for drinks or a bite to eat. With a downstairs toilet, what point was there in going upstairs?

I look around for a loft hatch. There isn't one. There are three doors off the hallway, all of them closed. I listen behind each one. I can't even picture the video now. Was it definitely a loft? Could it have been a storage room or spare room? No, it was definitely a loft. I swear I remember seeing rafters and a skylight. Then I notice another set of stairs above the ones I've just climbed. I can only imagine they lead to the loft.

I run up those stairs, too, and get to the top. There's just a brown wooden door, standing stern and solid. Nothing else. It looms in front of me, the last barrier stopping me from finally being able to get my daughter back. I yell Ellie's name and hear her call 'Daddy'. In that instant, my heart explodes and shatters. The adrenaline is coursing through my veins, making it hard to breathe. Everything has closed down to complete tunnel vision. All I can see is the door in front of me, and I visualise Ellie standing behind it, terrified. I tug at the handle and shoulder-barge the door, but it's not moving.

'Stand right away from the door, sweetheart,' I shout. 'I'm coming in.' I try to make my voice sound strong and confident, but it feels like electricity is flowing through me and I realise I sound like an adolescent schoolboy.

I'm mere seconds away from getting my daughter back. From ending this whole situation. My legs feel like jelly, but I know I need to summon up the strength and power to get through this door first. It's the last thing I have to do.

As I step backwards ready to throw myself at the door, Emma wraps her arm around my neck. For a moment, I feel my windpipe crunch slightly, and my instinct is to react. It all happens within a split second. Without even thinking, I grab her arm and pull it downwards, the adrenaline surging through me as I wrench her arm around and hear the shoulder pop like a cork gun at a funfair.

She yowls in pain as I let go and instinctively bend my leg at the hip and kick backwards, feeling my boot connect with her stomach before there's nothing – just air and silence, until the sickening thud as her head hits the wall on the landing at the bottom of the attic stairs. It feels like minutes, but it can only have been a second or two at most.

There's silence.

Instantly I know she won't be coming round from hitting her head this time. I don't need to look to know that – not having heard the sound – but I do. Her eyes stare forward, empty and glassy, as the blood trickles from her nostrils. There's pain on her face. Not physical pain, but pure sorrow and anguish. Her soul looks empty.

I don't even stop to think about how I'm going to explain this or what it means for me. It doesn't matter. There's only one thing on my mind right now. Only one thing that matters, that means more than anything else in the world. I throw everything I've got at the door. Once, twice. My shoulder is screaming, the pain shooting up and down my arm and across my back. I ignore it. No pain right now can be greater than the thought of coming so close and not being able to get Ellie back. Finally, on the third barge, the door gives.

It takes a second for everything to adjust. For the sound of the door splintering open to stop echoing around the loft space. For the dust to clear. For my eyes to get used to the light in here.

The room's dark, save for a glowing yellow lightbulb that hangs from one of the rafters. In the corner, I see a pair of scared, tired eyes looking out from behind a cardboard box. She looks so confused. Petrified, puzzled and weary all at the same time. My heart melts.

'It's okay, sweetheart,' I say, trying to sound as calm and reassuring as I can. I'm anything but calm inside, but I know I need to stop Ellie from worrying or panicking. She's probably been through so much of that already this week. The thought breaks my heart. 'It's me. It's Daddy.' My voice cracks as I speak. I swallow, trying to fight back the tears from my eyes.

As I move over to the boxes, Ellie crawls out and slowly stands up before walking over and wrapping her arms around my legs. We stand like that for a good minute or so, not wanting to let go, before I bend down and pick her up.

I look into her eyes and see that the scared, tired look is starting to fade. It's gradually being replaced with a look of happiness and the sort of childhood contentedness that adults no longer feel. She looks so tired. But she knows it's me. And she knows she's safe.

The overwhelming feeling is one of serene familiarity. The dead weight of my tired daughter, the warmth of her soft skin, her unique scent. They're all things I've missed, all things I've dreamed of. All things I never thought I'd experience again.

In that moment, everything feels right again. Despite Emma lying dead at the foot of the stairs, my marriage falling apart and the police trying desperately to pin whatever they can on me, none of that matters. I'll take all that and more just for the fact that I've got Ellie back. That's all that matters. That's all that ever mattered.

As we head for the door and down the stairs towards where Emma's body is lying, I pull Ellie into me, burying her face in my shoulder. She doesn't need to see that. She's been through more than enough without needing to know how it ended. All she needs to know is that she's safe and she doesn't need to worry about anything ever again. I'm going to make sure of that.

When we get outside, the cold night air whips against my skin and I feel spots of rain landing on me. Whereas at any other time this would feel like hell, I don't mind one bit. For the first time in a long time, I can feel again.

60

NICK

When I got home, I called the police. The walk home gave me plenty of time to think about what I was going to say.

I told them I went over to Emma's. I said she made a move on me and I heard noises coming from the loft. I said that Emma tried to stop me going up and we fought. She fell and hit her head. Twice. Bizarrely, this was the bit the police had trouble believing. Sometimes it's weird how the truth can be stranger than fiction.

As far as the police are concerned, that all adds up. They have no inkling that I tried to kill Tasha. The only real chance of that happening was extinguished with the light in Emma's eyes. I don't know if the whole Jen Hood thing will ever come to light. I presume not. I can't see any reason why Emma would have kept those emails on her computer. For all I know, she was using internet cafés, too. She's had this planned for so long, I'm pretty sure she will have covered her tracks better than I did.

Tasha has been her usual stoical self over the whole thing. I can never really tell what she's thinking. I doubt if I ever will.

McKenna's sitting on the sofa opposite me and Tasha, whilst Ellie sits, oblivious, in front of the cartoons on TV. As far as she's concerned, it's just another day.

'We found some old photos,' McKenna says. 'Quite a few, actually. One of the upstairs rooms was virtually a shrine, Nick. There were hundreds of photos of you and Emma from your university days, as well as some of the three of you. Tasha's face was . . . Well, let's just say removed from most of them. She had a diary, too. Most of it's about the two of you. Her obsession with you. We still haven't had time to go through it all yet, though.'

I swallow. 'She was keeping a diary? Recently?'

'She stopped about five and a half years ago, it seems. Around the time you would have announced your pregnancy. But I can't go into any more details at the moment, I'm afraid, until we've had a chance to look at it properly.'

'No, I understand,' I say. 'I'm just glad it's all over. I appreciate you tying up the loose ends, though.'

'There is one other thing,' she says. 'Derek Francis. In Emma's . . . room . . . we found more. She'd photocopied pages from her diary back when she was a schoolgirl. We haven't found the original yet, but that's only a matter of time. In it, she wrote about how Mr Francis had invited her into his house and begun sexually assaulting her over a course of months. To me, that explains why she was so damaged as a person. And she'd been using that to blackmail him.'

My mouth hangs open. 'That's why he told you he hadn't seen me put Ellie in the car. She had him over a barrel.'

'Exactly. And it explains why he's been so wary and suspicious of you all these years. He would've seen Emma coming and going from yours every now and again and realised how close to the wind he was sailing.'

'Jesus Christ. Is he going to be charged?'

McKenna raises her eyebrows momentarily and exhales. 'The problem with that is there's no-one to bring about a charge or make a complaint. We can't simply take a dead woman's diaries at face value. The defence counsel would have a field day if after all this we tried to convince a jury that Emma's words were those of a sane, rational-minded person. If she were alive to press charges and stand up in court herself, perhaps, but . . .' She leaves the thought hanging there in the air like a bad smell. 'And I think it's only fair to assume that she was behind your mugging, too, Tasha. It's the only thing we can assume, and without Emma around to testify otherwise that's going to be the assumption I'll make.' McKenna looks at me as she says this. A small part of me thinks that perhaps there's some hidden subtext behind her words. 'On that subject, by the way, the phone company were very helpful. They used triangulation to track where your phone had been. It turns out you did take it with you when you were walking through the park,' she says to Tasha, but looking at me. 'But it was switched off just after the attack, about forty yards further across the park. Looks as though whoever did it was heading towards the canal.'

I know what she's thinking, but she also knows that there's no way it could have been me who attacked Tasha. And as far as she's concerned, I had no reason to want to. She just knows something isn't quite right.

I break eye contact with McKenna to look back at Ellie, who's still transfixed by the cartoons on the screen. I just hope to God that she grows up to forget this whole ordeal and to become a confident, well-rounded person. More like her mother. Because I've got to admit it – perhaps being the shy, retiring one isn't always the best way to be.

Moments later, the cartoon programme finishes and I can sense Ellie starting to get grouchy. I smile a little as I recognise those signs that used to make me groan inwardly. The fidgeting, the tiredness in her eyes. All things that used to drive me mad, knowing I was about to have to deal with a stroppy toddler, but now make me glad to have her back.

I stand and walk into the kitchen, leaving McKenna and Tasha talking. I open the cereal cupboard and take out the Rosie Ragdoll, looking at it for a moment. Its eyes seem to have lost their human sparkle. It doesn't freak me out half as much as it used to. I close the cupboard door and head back into the living room. When I get there, I crouch down and hand Ellie the Rosie Ragdoll. Her beaming smile melts my heart, and it pains me that anyone could have wanted to harm her in any way.

I think on that for a moment. It's upsetting that anyone had to die for me to get Ellie back, but I knew that would have to be the case early on, as soon as I got the emails from Jen Hood. It was almost inevitable. I think about how close I came. The radio in the bath. The attack in the park. I think about what would've happened. What the ramifications would have been.

I kick myself now that I could have even considered being so stupid. If you're crazy enough to kidnap a child, you don't suddenly just become perfectly normal again once your blackmail victim has done what you want. And besides, that wasn't what she really wanted anyway. She wouldn't have just handed Ellie over and let us get on with our lives. She made it perfectly clear that she wanted us to be together. That had been her plan from day one. Would I ever have been truly free? No. I would have had to somehow let her down gently – again – and potentially make things even worse. I'm pretty good at making bad situations worse as it is, but that would have been something else.

I've got visions of living in the shrine in her upstairs bedroom, handcuffed to a steel-framed bed while she fawns over me and tells me that I'm hers now. I consider myself to have had a very lucky escape. Perhaps the perfect murder wasn't so difficult after all.

EPILOGUE

NICK

They say a leopard never changes its spots, but I don't know about that. I'm certainly not the person I once was, and even Tasha's spots have started to fade into light smudges. I guess they couldn't not. How can your priorities not change after something like that?

I almost had the shock of my life when she came to me a few days after Ellie's return and told me she was going to cut down her working hours and only work part-time from the office, doing the rest of her hours at home. I'm not sure I'm keen on her being around the house the whole time, but I know it's going to be better for Ellie. I'm just grateful that she's put someone else first for a change. After all those years that I wanted her to cut down her work and spend more time with me and Ellie, I really can't complain now that she's doing it – and off her own back, too. Maybe I'll have to reactivate that gym membership in order to get some me time.

She seems happier just for making the decision. Even though she won't be working her new hours until the end of the month, it's almost as if a huge black veil has been lifted from over her head. I can see life in her eyes again.

It feels like a different family unit now. I won't go as far as to say the world is a bright and sunny place again, but things have certainly changed. The first Sunday after Ellie came home, we went out for an afternoon walk. Just like we always used to. Tasha suggested going to the woods, but I told her I wasn't keen. *Best not to pretend we're the same people as we were*, I said. Better to make a clean break of it. So the woods are out of the equation, which suits me just fine. It works well. Things have never been ideal in the past, and I know we won't live a perfect life in the future. But it feels as though Tasha and I have both learned things. Many were things we didn't want to learn, but we needed to.

I don't want to jump the gun, but I think Tasha's finally learned that caring for your family doesn't mean spending all day in a stuffy office in order to add another zero to our bank balance. She never would have had it before what happened, but I really think cutting down her hours and spending more time at home is going to give her a far bigger feeling of self-worth. It'll bring us closer together as a family, too. Maybe I'm getting ahead of myself, but I can only hope.

I think we've all been changed by what happened. We couldn't not have been. Sure, Tasha isn't perfect. Far from it. But I know I'm not, either. I keep thinking back to that night that I told Emma I was leaving her for Tasha. It was the chain of events that kicked off everything that has happened since, but it also meant I dodged a bullet that night. As much as Tasha pisses me off sometimes, I could have ended up with someone like Emma.

What amazed me the most was how quickly the media attention died down. When Ellie came home, a number of news outlets got in touch to ask us to tell our story, but we were quick to point out that we wouldn't be doing any interviews now or in the future, so don't bother asking again, thankseversomuch. Probably not ideal for a writer to be turning down free publicity, but that's not the sort of media attention I'm after. That chapter is closed.

I'd be lying if I said that book sales hadn't picked up. My old publisher even did a new print run on *Black Tide*. It'll earn me the square root of bugger all in royalties, but there's the possibility that it might help me land a new deal with another publisher at some point in the near future. At least there's light at the end of the tunnel.

Tasha's parents, thankfully, never did make the trip over from Australia. Instead, they suggested that they should come over to us for Christmas this year. They'd love to come back to England again, they said, but as they're getting old they wouldn't want it to be a flying visit, so suggested staying for a month. I very kindly said that if they're worried about the travelling, we'll go over to them instead. For a fortnight.

We've decided we all need a holiday, too. I was really looking forward to lying on a beach for a couple of weeks, feeling the sea lapping at my toes. Sunlight is always good for recharging the batteries. Tasha, though, had other ideas. So we're off to Switzerland later in the year for a camping holiday. I've never been camping in my life, nor has she, but she was convinced that she wanted to do something a little more low-key. I'm not going to argue.

One thing that did surprise me was how accepting she was of my story about the gambling losses. I thought she would have completely destroyed me over it. I was convinced she was going to make me feel small and insignificant. A failure. I would have put money on it. As it happens, it all completely passed her by without so much as a raise of the eyebrows. I guess she's got other priorities now. Who wouldn't be happy to lose three grand if it meant getting your daughter back? I almost killed for her. I did kill for her, some might say. Personally I'm keen to keep my conscience clean. I've had enough of feeling bad about myself and worrying about my past.

I guess it put everything into perspective for both of us. Life isn't about the daily grind, the school-gate gossip, the keeping up with the

Joneses. Because all that shit will never go away, even if you want it to. The only things you can truly lose are those that are closest to you. And they're the things you don't want to lose.

Are we closer as a family now? Yes, undoubtedly. Are there things still left unspoken which are going to crop up at some point? Absolutely. I can almost guarantee it. Once the dust has settled, I know Tasha will have some questions to ask. But I also know that whatever my answer is won't matter. Because none of it truly matters. Not really.

Derek came over a few days after Ellie came home. I couldn't believe it when I saw him standing there on the doorstep. I've never once seen him cross the threshold at the foot of his drive. He just stood there for a few moments, looking down at the doormat. I could tell something was on his mind, so I asked him what was wrong. All he said was 'I'm so sorry.' He looked truly desolate. It's hard to find sympathy for a man who lied to you and lied to the police and almost had you arrested for kidnapping your own child, and it's even harder when you later find out the man's got a history of abusing children.

There was more silence after he said that, but I could tell he had more to say. So I just stood and watched him for a while. I didn't mind that he clearly felt uncomfortable. Why should I? Eventually, he spoke. He told me that he thought I might like to know that he'd put his house up for sale that morning. He wanted to tell me before I saw the 'For Sale' sign go up. I thanked him for coming to tell me and I wished him well for the future. It took a lot of strength and tongue biting to do that, but I managed it. I was proud of myself. I'm not sure how much of a future he has. He looked worn, twenty years older than he did a week before. I guess our pasts all catch up with us at some point, no matter how much we might think we've got away with it.

Am I naïve enough to think that it's plain sailing from here on in? No, of course I'm not. But I'm just grateful that we've at least got a fighting chance.

ACKNOWLEDGEMENTS

I tend to write books very quickly, but *Her Last Tomorrow* had me stumped for quite a while.

It began as a nugget of an idea and developed into a plot. One thing I didn't have, though, was an ending. Rather, I did have an ending but I couldn't find a way of weaving it into the existing plot in a way which I was happy with.

I spent a few months discussing the book every now and again with my wife (during which time I wrote and published two other novels) until I finally managed to get it right. As a result, primary thanks have to go to my wife for helping this book actually see the light of day. Without her input, it might still be stuck in a drawer somewhere.

I must also thank Lucy Hayward, who did a sterling job on feeding back her views on the story and plot and helping to polish *Her Last Tomorrow* for the first edition, which was published independently in December 2015.

That edition went on to be hugely successful and resulted in Amazon approaching me early in 2016 with a view to taking the book on under their Thomas & Mercer wing. For that, I need to thank Jane

Snelgrove, my editor at Amazon Publishing, for her support, advice and impeccable taste in books.

Thank you to Charlotte Herscher, my developmental editor at Amazon, for her extraordinary diligence on working with me to help develop *Her Last Tomorrow* into the book you've just read. I really don't like editing at all, but Charlotte made what would otherwise be a daunting prospect (adding 30,000 words and making a number of substantial changes within a short time frame) very workable indeed. It also has the added advantage that if you spot any mistakes, I can blame her.

The whole team at Thomas & Mercer have been fantastic and very supportive, so I need to thank them all. There are too many to name, but they know who they are.

Huge thanks must go to David Parry, formerly a detective sergeant with Leicestershire Police, for his insightful and in-depth advice on policing methods and procedure. My thanks also go to those police officers and detectives who provided me with additional information and fact checking but would prefer not to be named here.

Thanks also to Dave Whitelegg, one of the UK's foremost IT security experts, for his information on the dark web.

And thank you to you, the reader, for buying this book and (hopefully) enjoying it. Many people forget that the most important and vital people in an author's career are the readers, but I'm acutely aware of the fact that I wouldn't be typing this if it weren't for you.

READ FREE BOOKS AND SHORT STORIES BY ADAM CROFT

Thank you for reading *Her Last Tomorrow*. I hope it was as much fun for you as it was for me writing it. To say thank you, I'd like to offer you additional books and short stories. All members of my VIP Club have access to exclusive books and short stories which aren't available anywhere else. Membership is free and you can leave at any time, no questions asked.

To join the club, head to adamcroft.net/vip-club and two free books will be sent to you straight away.

I also love hearing from my readers, so please do get in touch with me if you'd like to. You can contact me via my website adamcroft.net, Twitter @adamcroft, or Facebook www.facebook.com/adamcroftbooks.

ABOUT THE AUTHOR

Adam Croft is a British author, principally of crime fiction, best known for the Kempston Hardwick Mysteries and his Knight & Culverhouse thrillers. In 2015, *Her Last Tomorrow* quickly became one of the biggest-selling self-published books of the year.

Adam regularly takes part in discussions and panels on publishing and the future of books, and was featured by the *Guardian* in 2016 as a top-selling self-published author.

His work has won him critical acclaim as well as four Amazon bestsellers, with his Kempston Hardwick Mysteries being adapted into audio plays starring some of the biggest names in British TV.

